MOUNTAIN BLOODBATH

Hoofbeats sounded through the camp. A rider urged a galloping horse among the tents. As the mount bore down, a shot boomed out. One man screamed and dropped his tomahawk. His face became a sheet of blood.

His rifle discharged, Pike drew his heavy pistol and triggered. The slug drilled into the throat of another outlaw trapper. The wound was fatal and the man fell, but his *compadres'* guns blazed on all sides. Hot lead whizzed past the big mountain man as he jumped from his saddle onto the hard ground, knife in hand, ready to do battle man-to-man!

MOUNTAIN JACK PIKE

#13 HIGH COUNTRY CLIMAX

JOSEPH MEEK

PINNACLE BOOKS
WINDSOR PUBLISHING CORP.

Yet another one for Marilyn

PINNACLE BOOKS

are published by

Windsor Publishing Corp.
475 Park Avenue South
New York, NY 10016

First Printing: April, 1993
Printed in the United States of America

Prologue

I

The gutted trout, as it cooked over the campfire, didn't smell merely tasty, it smelled *warming*. Or so thought Jack Pike, as he hunkered, shivering, over the low blaze in the depths of the canyon at dusk. One big hand gloved with otter skin wrapped the stick on which the fish was skewered, and the other rested on the frosty ground, steadying the mountain man's bulky frame. A few paces away gurgled the stream he'd made camp beside after a hard day of down-slope riding.

He huddled deeper into his woolen blanket coat. The chill in the air heralded the coming of winter, although no snow had fallen yet to make rough going of the trails through the passes. But Pike faced at least another day on horseback before he'd be down out of this rugged, treacherous range called the Bitterroots.

All that he could do was hope his luck would keep holding.

Pike exhaled, and a cloud of condensation flowed downward over his unruly beard. In the gathering gloom, his horse cropped grass where it was tethered beside a sheer wall of granite that loomed over the camp. The dun stallion's monotonous *chomp-chomps* sounded crisp and distinct—like all noises at this high altitude.

When a branch snapped in the nearby cedars, both man and horse reacted instantly. The dun pricked up its ears, while Pike tossed aside the fish and dove from the fire-lit circle. As he hit the ground and rolled, he managed to grab his primed, ready-to-fire Hawken rifle. Coming up in a crouching battle stance, he thumbed the flintlock's hammer to cock.

Pike's wary eyes spotted movement at the clearing's edge: someone was edging between him and the fire, and it was no Indian—too much noise was being made. Crouched in the shadows with the patience of a hunter, Pike waited for the hand to play out.

The silhouetted form strode over to Pike's horse, stretched a hand out to grab the braided tether.

"Oh, no you don't, fella! That's my mount you're trying to steal."

Pike flung from concealment, throwing the Hawken to his shoulder. But the stranger sensed the same thing Pike did: that a shot now could as easily kill the horse as the thief. The dun stud fiddlefooted, then reared, and Pike took advantage of the opportunity to rush the stranger. He drove into his opponent's midsection, and the pair went down kicking and punching.

The mountain man's face was clawed, his beard was yanked. Then he climbed on top, straddled his squirming opponent and bunched his fist to end it with a mighty blow. But when he pressed on the downed one's chest, his other hand dug softness.

A high-pitched gasp rang out.

What in hell? Breasts? Big mamas? The front of the thief's shirt parted, and two well formed melon-sized globes thrust into view. The bare skin gleamed like pale satin, puckered pink buds fused to taut cone-shaped tips.

"Y-you bastard!" the woman gasped. A sob caught in her throat.

"You're a *she*?" Pike scowled with scant sympathy. She'd intended to leave him afoot, a hundred miles from nowhere.

"*Of course*, I'm a woman! And at my wits' end, let me tell you! Alone, trying to get away from the man who made me run from him! Why, when I saw your fire, I—"

Pike grabbed her shoulder and dragged her closer to the fire. In the better light he studied the mussed blond hair and features that, although bruised, were more striking than he'd seen for quite a while.

He snapped at her: "You'd have made off with my stud horse. How did you expect to get along, way out in these woods?"

She stopped struggling, and a bewildered look came over her. When she spoke, her voice sounded more collected than it had a moment before. "You know, you're right. I wasn't thinking about the person the horse belonged to. Only my own self." Her slender fingers tried to hold closed the front of her man's shirt, but failed, due to the thrust of her remarkable bosom. But she went right on explaining herself. "I was scared, and that's the truth." Then she peered at him close-range, her cornflower blue eyes pleading. "But I won't be any more trouble to you, mister. I swear."

Pike, listening to her, felt his anger cooling. It appeared the woman had been in a bad fix. He bent and retrieved his rifle from where it had fallen. As far as he could see, the woman was weaponless. "All right, I'll trust you," he grunted. "You said something about a fella on your trail. Is he close behind?"

She shook her head: "No. Quite a way back, actually. I lost him yesterday. Hid in a tree until he gave up and rode off, cussing."

"You must be hungry," Pike said. "See that half-raw fish on the ground? What say we stir up the flames, finish cooking it and make us a meal?"

"You're inviting me to eat? Lordy! Thanks!" She smiled, and showed a row of strong, white teeth. "Here, let me hold the skewer."

"*I'll* toast the fish," Pike said, smiling for the first time since she'd shown up. "Now there's two of us, we'd best make the grub stretch, though. You'll find some old biscuits, an onion and a dented pot in my saddlebag."

"I'll look for 'em. By the way, Jenny Henderson is my name—born and raised back east in Sandusky. You can call me Jenny, Mr.—er?"

"Pike."

"Mr. Pike."

She rummaged in Pike's possibles poke, found the items that the mountain man had asked for. Since she had no covering on her head, the chilly breeze blew the long pale hair around her face. "Oh, while you're there," Pike called, "you may's well grab the horse blanket to wrap yourself."

Jenny did so, and returned to the fire shrouded and warmer-looking. Where the blanket's folds ended, Pike could see long, slim legs that were cased in man's canvas pants.

A few minutes later, the woman and Pike sat side by side, stuffing forkfuls of juicy trout into their mouths. "Pike, you're sure different from Abner Walsh, who I ran out on, account of he treated me bad. *He'd* never have cared I was cold. He'd make me serve his meals, fetch his jug, so he could eat off by his lonesome. That's besides pleasuring himself on me so rough. And beating me up."

She touched the bruised cheek Pike had noticed earlier.

"Did he hit on you often?"

She bobbed her chin. "That's what made me desperate. Before spending those weeks with Ab, I'd never have got it in my head to steal. And now, look! I got to thank you again, Pike, treating me so nice after what I tried—"

"Jenny," Pike said, "damned if you aren't looking a mite tuckered!" He wasn't much for sitting and listening to compliments. "What say we turn in, the fire between our two bedrolls? Let it burn a spell for warmth and to scare away bears."

9

Jenny straightened, and her eyes grew round. "Bears? I'm scared of bears."

"Reckon folks don't see many, back in Sandusky."

Pike came awake knowing he'd not slept long: the coals of the fire still glowed a dull cherry red. His eyes picked out the source of the noise that woke him: Jenny was standing over his bedroll, wriggling her body as she worked to push down her britches. When she'd shed this last garment and kicked it away, her naked form gleamed in the moonlight.

Her body was everything a man could ask: heavy breasts over a wide rib cage, well-fleshed legs, the dense mat of pale hair at her vee. The scent of her heat reached Pike's nostrils, and his penis started to grow. He was going to say something, but before he could she'd slid under the soogans and pressed herself against him. "Pike, I got to thinking of those bears. I'm trembling. Can you feel me tremble?"

He grinned. "Sure can."

"Say! Why, you're wearing clothes under the covers!"

"The air's chilly."

She sniffed. "What you need, Pike, is a better way to keep warm. Let's see what I can do about it!"

She worked and tugged at his buckskins' tie strings. When she'd slid the shirt from his muscle-slabbed torso, her hands moved to his midsection.

She froze when her fingers brushed the big Kentucky pistol stuffed in his waistband.

10

"Lordy!"

"Easy, gal. It's the gun that's saved my life more times than I care to mention."

He slid the weapon outside the blanket and laid it on a rock.

Meanwhile, Jenny's hand had been stroking his cock. "Now, *here's* something hard that I can appreciate!"

He glued his mouth to hers, cupped a breast in his callused palm, flogged her nipple with his thumb. Her whole body quivered in ecstasy. Invitingly, Jenny arched her back and parted her thighs.

Her crevice was warm, wet and oh so ready. As his swollen gristle probed the portal of her love passage, she clamped her legs about his waist. They began to rock in the age-old motion. "Oh, God, Pike," she moaned in a whiskey voice. "I need this like a thirsty man needs water! Don't stop!"

He didn't aim to.

Now their locked bodies bucked more violently. Her movements were those of a rutting wildcat. Her groans became mewing animal cries. "Yes, Pike! Yes! Oh, yes!" she cried. She rode with him through a series of small, galvanic orgasms, then screamed outright as an earthquake of utter pleasure tore through her body. Pike's blood rushed through his veins.

At the crest of both their passions, his seed boiled out and into her.

A wave of deep relaxation flowed over the man. The spent pair lay awhile on their backs, sweating and letting the minutes spin out. Gradually, their breathing returned to normal. Pike shifted a bit and heard her murmur: "Stay still and just let me snuggle. Let's sleep."

They slept.

II

Later, they were roused by the call of a hoot owl. Jenny Henderson opened her eyes, and found the big man's gaze drinking her in. "How do you feel, Pike?" She looked like the cat who'd gotten the cream. "Let me tell you, *I* feel great. I needed what you gave me—every wonderful inch."

"I thought it was good, too, Jenny."

Her leg rested comfortably in his groin as they chatted.

"You've got to be one of the best of the mountain-man breed, Pike. That's my notion, but I'm sure of it, even though I haven't been in the West long." She paused a minute, as if deciding how much to say. "Not that I don't know something of the out-doors—my pa was a farmer, and he taught me to use a gun, shoot varmints in our corn patch and the like." A smile. "When I left home to make my own way, I took to earning a living in a more fun way. Ended up at Fort Graybull last July. That's where I met Ab, the no-good. D'you know, *he* called himself a mountain man. But he's nothing like you, Jack Pike."

By Pike's reckoning, she'd probably told him more than she thought. For example, that she'd worked as a whore. A few weeks before, Pike had crossed paths with old Wasatch Smith, and the crusty trapper had dropped word of the four new and pretty "soiled doves" who'd arrived at the trading post on the Yellowstone. It wasn't hard to guess the rest: Jenny must have attached herself to Ab Walsh, not realizing what she was getting into.

Pike had tangled with the rough-spoken Arkansan a time or two. The man was notorious for abusing women and horses.

"It must be great to make a living trapping in the high country, Pike. The snowcapped peaks, the forests up here are magnificent."

Pike lay back, clasping his hands behind his head. "It isn't a bad life, else I wouldn't do it. And up in the Shining Mountains, as we call 'em—well, the freedom makes up for the danger. Matter of fact, I'm about ready to go on back up, spend the winter in a beaver valley I've had my eye on. On my way to Graybull first, though, for stocking up on supplies. Once the big snows come, forget about the trails. They're well-nigh impassable."

Her voice turned eager. "Mind if I keep company with you as far as the post, Pike? I don't get along well by myself in the wild—that you've seen."

Pike stroked his beard. "I reckon that'd be all right. But I can't make promises beyond getting you there. I'm to meet my longtime pard, Skins McConnell, at Graybull, and soon as we can, we'll be heading out together. That's the pact we made last summer, Jenny."

"Pike, I don't expect you to go on taking care of me forever!" She squeezed his manhood, playfully at first, but soon Pike felt her breathing grow husky and rapid.

"You feel all right, gal?"

"I feel grateful to be lying next to you this way! Let me show you *how* grateful!"

Her hands—both of them—were kneading his gristle, which by now was rock hard. He rolled on top and entered her, and she half screamed: "Ah-aah-*aah*, Pike! Thatta way! Thatta way!"

It was shaping up as one hell of a fine trip, this one to Fort Graybull.

Part One
The Threat

Chapter 1

The last day that Pike and Jenny spent coming down out of the foothills, they trailed under tree limbs that were rapidly dropping leaves, clawing the sky like blackened dead men's hands. The man and woman felt their faces stung by chill north winds, and as they left wooded steeps, the flats stretched ahead, all brown and bare of summer graze. Not wanting the dun to have to carry double, the man and woman took turns in the saddle. Jenny was young, healthy and strong, and Pike didn't feel he was being slowed down.

Now as they trudged up the last rise before coming upon Graybull, Pike's nose caught scents of the outpost, most of them unpleasant to him. Human odors mingled with animal smells—and, of course the overriding smell of wood smoke.

"We're almost there," called Pike over his shoulder to the woman aboard the horse. "Inside there'll be stoves to sit by and get warm. As for me, I plan a big dose of sipping whiskey."

"Sounds good, Pike. Real good."

She was smiling in the way that Pike had gotten used to in recent days. He looked back fondly on the bedroll romps they'd shared; still, he knew he'd be relieved to get her off his hands. There'd be plenty to keep him busy in the days ahead: making plans with McConnell, teaming up to put his and his friend's outfits in shape. They'd need to pick out a place to winter—maybe Lemhi Valley or the wilder and harder-to-reach Eagle Valley, where beavers still abounded.

And with the onset of cold weather, there wasn't much time left to waste. Pike's sixth sense told him that the season's first big snowfall wouldn't be long in coming.

Fort Graybull, from a distance, resembled a cluster of toys set down by a giant hand in the shadow of the mountains. The adobe walls topped with a palisade of pointed logs looked almost fragile, and adjoining stock pens, sheds and lean-tos were just as ugly as Pike remembered them. The smoke from a number of chimneys trailed dark smudges across the low, gray sky.

"I don't see any people—none," Jenny said.

"Nobody there's caught sight of us yet. I'll fire a shot and let 'em know we're coming." Pike tilted the Hawken up, eared the hammer with his thumb and triggered. The gun's lockspring propelled the flint down against the frizzen, and sparks showered into the firing pan.

Boom.

"Why spend powder and ball that way?" Jenny asked.

"A habit a mountain man gets, letting folks know when he's riding in. Seems it's expected."

"But there still aren't any people in the fort showing."

She had a point: although the gate to the trading post stood open, and horses could be seen standing in the compound, not one human being was in evidence.

"Damn!" Pike swore. "If something isn't wrong, I'll eat my hat!"

Pike tramped through the gate, the woman following aboard the walking dun. By the number of mounts either standing at hitch rails or ground-picketed—most still wearing saddles—Pike reckoned that a brigade of fur men had arrived not long since. He'd found out, over the years, that he seldom got along with the organized bands of men employed by the fur companies. By the same token, brigade men didn't get on well with free trappers—like Pike.

Now to Pike's ears came shouts, the crash of overturning, breaking furniture. The sounds came from the squat log building where, Pike knew, liquor was laid down for anyone with the coin or pelts for payment. The brawl seemed to have been going on a while. Since reloading his gun would take time, the big man thrust it at Jenny. "Hold onto this!" he barked. Then he was on the move, dashing to the door of the taproom. Shouldering inside, Pike found himself squinting against dimness and clouded tobacco smoke, and he saw that he'd guessed right. A number of rough-looking jaspers in buckskins had ganged up on one man. A man they'd trapped in a back corner.

A thrown bottle crashed into a wall near Pike's head. A near miss.

"Nev' mind th' newcomer!" a hoarse voice whooped. "Over there stands th' troublemaker!"

"Larn him Ludlow's Bay men rule the Bitterroots!"

Pike saw nobody looking like a trading-post employee—had the barkeep and all others fled?

Across the room, a fist met a face with a squishing sound

"Ow!"

A rawboned man, about as tall as Pike but less massive, broke from the crowd. This man drew back an arm, drove a fist into an adversary's breadbasket. The brigade man in filthy buckskins reeled backward, yelping in pain and drooling yellow vomit. Then the clean-cut one glanced Pike's way, and surprise lit up his eyes. "Jack, is that you?"

"McConnell? Skins McConnell?"

One of the brigade jaspers threw himself at the tall, lean trapper. Rope-like sinews corded McConnell's arm as he roundhoused to his attacker's chin. "Ain't this a helluva thing?" McConnell roared jubilantly. "Get me in a tough spot, and my old pard, Jack, shows up just in time to join in."

"Behind you, Skins! Look out!"

The wielder of a stoneware jug came high with the thing, then brought it down. McConnell raised his left arm to deflect the blow, then crossed with his right fist in a powerful punch. The Ludlow's Bay man's jaw crunched, his knees buckled, and he

20

sank soundlessly. By now Skins McConnell's foes sensed the newcomer was against them, too: about half their number—six—converged on Pike. Pike pumped a leg, kicking one in the gut, then caught another with an uppercut. This one fell back, hands over a mouth that leaked crimson. By now, McConnell, on the offensive, slammed the heads of two opponents together with a *thunk*. One victim spun away, upchucking a flood of trade whiskey.

"Just get in?" McConnell called to Pike over the affray. His fist smashed a nose, and its owner howled.

"Yeah. You?"

"Me, I got here yesterday. No trouble at all until a few minutes ago." McConnell snorted. "Goddamn bush-loper bastards took offense when I called 'em chicken shit."

The fighting ebbed and flowed, Pike taking a jab to the ribs, then McConnell's ear getting boxed, pain lancing into him. Pike sledged a fist into an opponent's paunch, and when the man jackknifed, he slammed his nose with a pumped knee. McConnell fended off a swung chair leg, exchanged punches with a bearded giant who wore a deerskin eye patch.

"Back 'em to th' wall!" the brigade man roared. "Mop the floor with 'em!"

The loudmouthed one was hairy and mean. Pike grabbed a beer bottle and flung it at the tough. The impact on his temple sent the victim reeling. McConnell fought back-to-back with Pike now, driving his elbow into the throat of a string-bean-thin adversary.

The low-ceilinged room rang with shouts.

"It's all of us 'gainst two of them!"

"Then, for Christ's sake, let's *kick* their asses!"

Mountain Jack Pike's bulky frame, standing a full six foot four, ranged the room, his meaty fists flailing. His horny knuckles impacted noses, cheeks and chins. His fists were as devastating as oak mallets.

A stumpy, stubble-chinned gent pulled a skinning knife. McConnell dropped to one knee, and diving under the toad stabber, powered a fist to the jaw of the foe. There was a rattling crunch of breaking bones. He caromed off the wall, and pitched to the sand-strewn floor, howling.

"They want to use weapons, do they?" Pike yelled.

"So it's more than just a fistfight!"

"Do it to them?"

"Hell, yes! And do it *right now!*"

Both trappers' hands dove under their coats. Out came the Kentucky pistols each carried, primed. The short guns, when glimpsed by the toughs, had an effect.

Suddenly the place was quiet. Injured Ludlow's Bay men sat or lay about on the floor, either unconscious and peaceful, or awake, with their faces screwed with pain. Those still on their feet cowered against the walls, hands elevated, snarling.

The heavy pistol was a drag on Pike's arm; still, he'd shot men with it often, and would do so again if someone looked crosseyed at him. "All right," he bellowed. "I know there's a barkeep within earshot! I want him to know I'm a friend of Tim Flanagan, owner of this post! So if you value your job, barkeep, come out of hiding and lend a hand!"

From behind a stack of liquor kegs a man stepped, his face pale and his hands twisting a

22

greasy apron. His weasel's mouth twitched. "Wasn't that I wanted the fight to go," he stammered. "But with the boss gone off, Dan'l—that's me—"

"You're not one against a dozen jaspers now, Dan'l. *We're* here. So go round up Flanagan's men from around the post—the cook, blacksmith, who-ever. Tell them they'd best have guns with 'em." Turning to the troublemakers: "I reckon you boys should take thought to leaving. And, yeah, I mean clear out of Fort Graybull."

"That's c'rect," said Skins, talking with a split lip. "Me and my pard, we aim to have a drink in private. So drag this scum"—he toed one of the downed men—"into the open. The air in here's sure got foul."

A red-bearded brigade man scowled. He shook a fist, the fringes of his buckskins flapping. "Ludlow's Bay is one *big* fur company, mister. There's more'n a hundred men in our brigade, camped over the first rise off to the east. Our booshway's one of Canada's best, Baptiste LeSage—tough enough to chaw rifle balls. Tangle with us, and you bite off more'n you can chew!"

Pike twitched his gun barrel. "Y'know, somehow it doesn't look that way."

"Our time, us and LeSage's will come!" The spokesman scowled. "Soon, when you and your friend McConnell ain't watchin' your backs."

"Git!"

Boots and moccasins shuffled. Hard-bitten crew members dragged companions to their feet and helped them stagger to the batwings. When the last limped across the threshold, Pike and McConnell peered through the window, sizing up the situation

23

outside. On the storage-shed roofs that doubled as ramparts, a half-dozen Graybull employees watched with rifles held ready. Even Dan'l stood with chin out and spine stiffened.

"What the barkeep claims is true," McConnell rumbled. "Tim Flanagan was away—on a buffalo hunt, I'm told—when I rode in. Dan'l was a weak stick to leave in charge, but I reckon Tim didn't foresee trouble."

"I reckon the brigade gents tried to crowd you?" Pike asked.

"Hell!" Skins snorted. "They dropped some insults about free trappers. The kind I'm proud to be."

Pike and Skins watched the company men's retreat. Just as they thought the last Ludlow's Bay man was out the gate, another sprinted from between two sheds, one hand waving. The jasper's other hand held up his patched wool pants.

"Fella's visit to the privy cut short?" Skins questioned.

Pike shrugged.

The runner caught up with the last rider, who reached down and helped his pard mount behind the saddle. Dan'l announced: "That's the last of 'em."

"Tell you what, Dan'l," Pike said. "We'll be at that table in the corner, pouring our own whiskey from a nice, fresh bottle. That way we won't get the crackskull meant for the Indians. Meanwhile, invite inside the party who rode in with me."

"The party who's holding your rifle?" McConnell's face wore a smirk.

"Yeah, my Hawken. I'd fired it earlier, had no chance to reload."

"It's a woman came with you, am I right?" Skins ventured.

"How'd you guess?"

McConnell elbowed his friend playfully. "You got the look, *compadre*. Like you've got laid lately. Us mountain men's eyes are sharp."

Pike squinted. "You noticed the neat mend in my coat, that's all. But you're right, I met a gal on the trail. I warn you, Skins, she's pretty, and when I introduce you, you may like her. Just don't you two drink the bottle empty. Fighting makes *me* just as thirsty as does you!"

Chapter 2

"So the Ludlow's Bay boys traipsed all the way down here from Canada! To throw their weight around? Looks like they mean business this time."

Pike gripped the bottle of Old Thunderbolt, splashed the booze into a bent tin mug as he peered across the table at McConnell. Sunshine beamed through the window of the taproom, brightening things up. Skins, sitting opposite his friend, nodded absentmindedly. His eyes were fixed on Jenny. The woman sitting next to Jack wasn't just good-looking, but in a merry mood from what she'd imbibed.

"I'd like to ask a question," she said. "Why the hard feelings? I mean, between you and those other men? Watching them ride out, I couldn't help but think they'd gone up against timber wolves. Are you rivals at trapping, maybe?"

"Not so much trapping as *trading*," Skins explained. "When a fella goes after pelts, the contest

26

is betwixt him and the beavers—and the weather and the wilderness. But the traders, they're dangerous in a different way. Some are downright cheats and thieves, laughing up their sleeves when they can leave a trapper with no cash for his season's work. And what with the beavers always getting scarcer—well, the companies get more greedy."

"It's like they want to make a last big killing," Pike put in. He quaffed his cupful. "You see, for years companies, one after another, have tried to corner the market. Sent brigades out, numbering in the hundreds, either to open new territories or take over established ones so as to squeeze out free trappers. Even the likes of Jim Bridger and Milt Sublette at times joined brigades. Later they saw the light and quit." He wiped his mouth with the back of his hand, and poured another drink. "Skins, you've heard of this booshway the Ludlow's Bay man mentioned?"

"LeSage? Sure."

"Me too," Pike said. "One tough Canadian. Maybe wolf-mean on account of his scarred face—"

"Talkin' about Baptiste?" rang out a loud voice. "Well, I've just come from him! So, me boyos, I know just where the man stands!"

The man who strode across the room was wiry and whang-tough, his head of flaming red hair above a face brown as an old saddle. "If it ain't Jack Pike and Skins McConnell! Ain't seen you for a spell, and damned if you ain't a sight for sore 'uns." He rested a long-barreled Sharps buffalo gun against the plank bar, then offered Pike his hand. They shook warmly. "And Miss Henderson, you're back, too! 'Tis a small world, begorrah!"

"Tim Flanagan, you old Irishman!"

"And an honest and fair-minded one!" Skins told Jenny.

"I know," she answered. "Mr. Flanagan, when I was here before, treated me kind."

"Didn't bring back no buffler hump," Flanagan griped, snatching up the bottle and swigging. "But I met some ornery bastards—the ones you boyos drove outa here. Aye, I had words with 'em." He ran fingers through his red thatch. "Ludlow's Bay, 'tis a big company. No trader can ignore 'em. And that LeSage, sent out to lead this brigade, he's one tough bastard."

"The feller's men ganged up to break my bones," Skins said.

Flanagan's face showed regret. "Had I been here, I would've *forced* hospitality." He cocked a thumb toward his rifle.

"Sit with us a bit, Tim," Pike invited.

In less than an eye-blink, Tim's bulk was sprawled in a chair, bandy legs outstretched. "I'd best come straight to the point. I need to palaver with ye, Pike, regardin' LeSage. Seems he's authorized to make me a buyout offer. Now, God knows, the idee of retirin' ain't come to me serious—"

"You once claimed you'd *never* sell," Skins reminded him. "Vowed to keep trading till time came to bury you."

"Hell, them's still me feelings!" The trader wagged his round head. "And the Ludlow's Bay's dollar offer? Chicken feed. But the damn truth is—" Flanagan's gaze dropped.

"Look here," Pike said. "Did this LeSage make

threats? Or even hint that you'd best sell, so's to save your hide?"

"That ain't it, Jack. Rather, 'twas a slow death he forecast for Graybull. Ludlow's Bay Company will lure the trappers away, keep 'em from bringin' their plews to me. Mind, I talked to LeSage briefly, when he hailed me at the edge of his camp. But he hinted plenty. By Christ, but his face is ugly!"

"It is that."

"The Canuck's face is badly scarred," Skins told Jenny. "He might've been mauled once by a bear. Although a rumor has it that Huron redskins captured him as a kid. And *they* put out one of his eyes and marked his cheeks. Only LeSage knows the facts."

Jenny wrinkled her nose in distaste.

Tim Flanagan was speaking again: "LeSage, he said he'd come here tonight for an answer. Ride over after sundown." A sigh. "Who can guess what he's up to? Got him a private army, a'most. Maybe he plans to brigade the territory, drive out the free trappers. Sendin' all the pelts east by his own means, he'd bypass me. Without pelts passin' through my hands, I'd go broke. My workers jobless, their families would be without grub."

Pike drank off his whiskey. "Sounds like a bluff to me, Tim. There's too many beaver valleys, too many free trappers. And your old customers—most of them—ought to stay loyal."

"Make that, 'might *want* to stay loyal.' Beaver men go where they can get top prices. They got to. Otherwise they can't buy powder, bullets, t'baccy—or replace old traps."

"That tears it!" Pike's hand slammed down, jarring the table. "Tim, you're not going to wait here. LeSage won't show till late—he'll aim to keep you in a sweat, wear out your nerves. What he hasn't banked on is *us* backing you. So here's what we'll do. You, me and Skins, we'll ride over to his camp. Tell him what for. The camp's over the ridge, you say?"

A nod from the trader.

"We'll start out now! Ready, Skins!"

"Ready!"

Flanagan looked grateful. "I'm obliged, fellers. You're makin' me feel like we can win this thing."

"Wait for us Jenny," Pike told the woman. "Make yourself at home. You know your way around the post—you stayed here before. We'll get this business settled, be back soon."

She hoped this rugged man was right.

Chapter 3

The sun hung poised in the afternoon sky when the three rode into the camp, horses trotting. Riding between his *compadres,* Pike let his eyes roam his surroundings. There was a belt of sturdy ash and cottonwoods that flanked a creek meandering down a prairie cleft. Tents lined the banks—lots of tents. In front of several, iron pots hung from tripods over buffalo-chip fires. The savory smell of antelope stew wafted.

Men with battered faces and torn clothes hunkered around the fires, glaring up at the arrivals. The losers in the taproom brawl weren't welcoming guests. Pike, McConnell and Flanagan reined in, and a burly man with a black beard stepped up. "What d'you jaspers want?"

Pike answered loudly. "Baptiste LeSage palavered with Mr. Flanagan, here, this afternoon. Said he'd have more things to say tonight. We've come to hear 'em."

Blackbeard squinted and thought. "I'll go and tell the boss he's got comp'ny." The man turned and went into a tent, emerged a moment later and beckoned. "This way, gents. 'Light down offa your horses and go in. LeSage ain't alone under canvas—he never is—so don't count on gettin' the drop. It's just his way of keepin' safe, y'see."

"Live by the sword, be scared of dying by the sword?"

The Ludlow's Bay man gaped stupidly. "Huh?"

"Never mind." Pike swung from the saddle, the Hawken in his grip. "All we'll do is what we came for."

Daylight shone through the sailcloth, and the tent's interior wasn't dim. A bedroll lay open in one corner, unoccupied. In the middle of the groundcloth stood three men, two of them muscular characters who looked dull-witted. The other man was their leader, the representative of the Ludlow's Bay Company's Western arm.

Baptiste LeSage was not a small man, and approached Jack Pike's own height, but without the chest girth. Aside from size, there was no comparison between the fellow with the French name and the mountain man. The pockmarked face of LeSage was marked by a scar that ran like a purple worm from scalp to jaw line. The left eye had been gouged out, and the empty socket was worn like a badge: a puckered hole, unconcealed by an eye patch. The hooked nose resembled a buzzard's beak.

"Mes amis!" LeSage rasped, although the man knew these visitors weren't friends. Still he chose to act cordial, for now. *"Messieurs* Flanagan, O'Connell and Pike, who I remember of old. Welcome to my prairie abode, so far from my homeland. You'll pardon the lack of chairs—"

"We don't mind standing," Pike said. "This won't take long." His companions, flanking him, nodded.

"Oh? Then *Monsieur* Flanagan is going to accept my company's price? What I'm authorized to offer for Fort Graybull? *Alors*—"

Pike nudged Tim. "Er, jes' the opposite, boosh-way," the trader said. "I *ain't* selling. Don't never aim to. Hell, the tradin' post's been my life."

The scarred man's mouth closed to a cruel gash. "Were I you, I wouldn't let the post *take* my life!"

"No threats," Pike put in.

LeSage raised a hand, palm outward. "What threat is in what I say, *monsieur?* I make a prophesy, that's all. Without the trading, a trader starves, not true? Threats? *Mon Dieu*, I need make no threats to Flanagan."

Pike scowled. "To who, then?"

LeSage glanced right, then left. His sidekicks looked hard enough to bite nails.

But they didn't scare Pike or Skins.

"Well-l-l—" LeSage continued. "That depends. The men in this camp, they've come a long distance from their stamping grounds. At great cost to the Ludlow's Bay Company, I add. And lately the head office has had much to say about return on costs." Fixing his eye on Flanagan: "It's a matter of profits, no? You, being a businessman, see."

Pike spoke up. "What *I* see is a lot of bullshit getting slung in this tent. Come on, *compadres*. We gave LeSage his answer."

The mountain man spun on his heel.

"Wait!"

Pike halted.

"Let me tell it more clear." LeSage grimaced, not grinned. "Let me describe a course of events. What *might* happen, despite anything you can do, Jack Pike. A year goes by, two years, and a pelt trader sees no pelts. The trappers, they no longer come. They're prevented from coming. Company men guard the mountain trails. Many well-armed men."

McConnell said, "You'd dry up the fur trade? Force the free trappers south? If your men stand guard, they're not trapping, so *you're* taking no furs. Packing out no pelts. That means no profits to Ludlow's Bay! What's good in that?"

"I never said there'd be *no* fur market."

"Oh?"

"Look outside this tent." LeSage threw back the entrance flap. The valley stretched away. "Water and wood. The mountains aren't too far off. For a new trading post, this is a fine spot, *non?* A new Ludlow's Bay enterprise." The Canadian sneered. "It won't take much to lure free trappers. Prices offered at Fort Ludlow will be good. There'll be safety from the dangerous Blackfeet."

" 'Tis true, the Blackfeet allus side with Ludlow's Bay." Flanagan groaned. "The Canadian founders bribed the tribe's chiefs years back. Today the outfit keeps on doin' it."

Pike faced LeSage. "We won't be bluffed, fella.

Flanagan keeps his post. You and Ludlow's Bay be damned!"

The booshway's ugly face flushed. *"Sacrebleu!* Get out of my tent! Oh, I know your reputation, Pike— as the mountain man trappers spin yarns about! But I'm betting you can be thrown out of this camp! I've men enough for that!"

"You may be right. Come on Skins and Tim." The mountain men and the trader exited, strode to their horses. Once in the saddle and trotting through falling dusk, they looked neither right nor left. As the lights of the trading post loomed out of the gloom, Pike growled, "The bastard."

"Shit, I oughtta have sold out," Flanagan muttered.

"Now you lost the chance," McConnell said. "Jack screwed up the deal *on purpose.* Why, Jack's got tricks up his sleeve! Ain't that right, Jack?"

Pike rode without speaking.

Skins told Tim, "He'll tell us, and we'll laugh our asses off. Tricks Jack's got. Can't be beat. You'll see."

Only Pike knew that his sleeves felt empty. Damned empty. He'd hated LeSage's gloating, and so shot his own mouth off. It wasn't his style to back down. So what to do next?

Maybe Flanagan's old friends *would* rally to him. But, on the other hand, maybe they'd drift away— or run scared. *Christ*, Pike wondered. *Who can know the future?*

Alongside him, Skins coaxed Tim to chuckle. *Reckon I'll need to do some heavy calculating.*

Chapter 4

Jenny Henderson sat at the taproom table, eating the supper of deer meat, beans and greens rustled up for her by the post cook. Beyond the window that looked westward toward the mountains, the last of day's color was leaching from the sky. She forked down her last mouthful and hailed the bar dog: "Dan'l, that room I stayed in before. Anyone using it these nights?"

The man smacked lips like a toad's. "Not that I know of, honey. But hey, you don't want to sleep by your lonesome there. Cracks in the walls and drafts." His sweaty hands compressed his bar rag. "Say, why don't I stop by later? Can't pay yer reg'lar fee for pleasurin' a man, but we can have fun!"

She frowned and tossed her yellow mane. "Thanks, but no thanks. I only do it for cash money. Ever since Ab Walsh."

She saw no point in mentioning Pike, with whom she'd disported for free, to their mutual delight. There was no comparison between Pike and this leering excuse. Dan'l McCue was more ferret than man.

The ferret dropped a wink. "Sure, Jen. Whatever you say. My time'll come." He scratched a hairy, pimpled arm.

"You go 'head, get your rest."

"Best advice I've had all day."

Out through the batwings the woman pushed. The air outside smelled fresh, without a whiff of spilled booze or stale spittoons. The stars were out, a million pinpricks on a black canopy. Jenny started walking, her coat wrapped tight against the chill. A couple of Flanagan's men passed her as they crossed the compound.

Soon Jenny was moving between two adobe buildings, the darkness inky. At the end of the passage she came to the door she sought, but the cubicle behind it was lit by a tallow candle.

"Hello! Who's here?"

Without warning, a blow fell across her spine: a wallop from a hickory spoke!

Damn!

Another blow struck her arm. Pain lanced.

Jenny Henderson fought back. She kicked behind her blindly, heard a harsh grunt. She tried to whirl and face her assailant, but was jumped on, the other person's weight collapsing her knees. Then both combatants hit the floor, kicking and squealing.

"Damn you! Damn you!" Jenny squawked, lashing out with her eyes squeezed shut. Her fist collided with her opponent's body, and a scream rang out: "Ow-w-w! Aa-ii-ii!"

Then came a thudding of feet cased in winter mocs—moccasins of buffalo-skin stitched with the hair inside. Jenny was grabbed again, and this time dragged from her adversary. Her wrists were pinned in a strong grip. Opening her eyes, she saw Jack Pike. Just a few paces away, McConnell was grappling with a slim figure in a muslin nightdress. The woman's breasts filled the bodice to almost breaking.

Jenny's attacker was a woman, and an attractive one.

She was about Jenny's age, with striking features and cascading sorrel hair. "Let me go," the redhead squawked, struggling.

Jenny stared in disbelief. "Flo? Is that you, Flo?"

"Good God! Jenny Henderson? I thought a thief was in my room! Why didn't you say it was only you?"

Pike released Jenny's arms, threw a glance at McConnell. "We busted up a catfight," he snapped.

McConnell shrugged. "A fella hears screams as he climbs down off his horse. So what does he do? He runs to the rescue."

"Oh-h-h, *you!*" Jenny pointed a finger at Flo. "Why didn't I tell you it was me when I walked in? You gave me no chance!" Her eyes flashed bolts like lightning, and her fists bunched. Then seeing the humor of things, she laughed in a rich contralto. "But what the hell? No use holding a grudge—not against you!"

Jenny sensed introductions were in order. "Flo,

meet Jack Pike. And his sidekick there is Skins McConnell. Both are fine-looking mountain men, as you can see. Pike and Skins, meet Flo Lipscomb. She and me, we're in the same line of work." She shrugged. "You may as well know the whole story. We 'ladies of the night' came west in the same wagon train. It was only after the conestogas rolled back east that we found we were stuck till next year."

The longer he looked at her, the more Skins liked the looks of Flo. She was extraordinarily trim, he saw through her nightdress fabric. Inside his pants, his cock had risen to attention. He wondered if the gals would notice.

They spotted the bulge at the same time. "Oh-oh! Look at that!"

"Flo, I *am* looking, honey. A feast for sore eyes!" Now Jenny's gaze turned to Pike, who wore a similar bulge.

"Why, how sweet! You're hard as a rail spike!" Pike's erection wasn't as conspicuous as Skins's. The mountain man's powder horn, slung by its thong, served a concealing function.

The men were eager, and so were the women. But the room held just one bed, its tick stuffed with last year's buffalo grass. Jenny linked arms with Pike, as Flo sidled to Skins's side.

"So," Jenny said. "How to handle this?"

Flo had an idea. "The next room's got a bed, same as this. A dandy crib." She fingered Skins's trousers front. "C'mon, Skins. Let's get on over there. Jawing's a waste of good time."

Skins didn't resist.

As soon as the other couple was gone, Jenny

pressed her body to Pike. Her cheeks were flushed. "So good to touch you again, Pike. Did things go well at LeSage's camp?"

"I'll tell you later, Jenny."

Pike was shucking out of his jacket, fringed elk-hide shirt and buckskin britches. When he dropped his wool balbriggans, his member flew up to slap belly flesh.

By this time, Jenny too was naked.

Pike's cock was stiff as a barber pole. The chilled skin of the woman's thighs was pink—the same shade as her pebbled nipples. Her perfect contours—wide shoulders, luxurious hips—were accented by the silky delta.

Pike maneuvered her to the bed, and they flopped down. Jenny's lips met Pike's, her tongue snakelike and darting. Pike hoisted her and she spread her legs to straddle his hips. Her juices smeared him with warm wetness.

Now his mouth found her pillowy breast, and the woman sighed. He fed on her like a cow on grass, first the right nipple, then the left. Her body writhed in pleasure as his mouth roamed down. "I'm on fire, Pike," she moaned in a husky voice, then the words became mere gaspings.

He played her like a fine fiddle, and in return she stroked his stalk, squeezed it. Drew it between her thighs, caressed it with buttery warmth.

"Lordy, Pike, but I've been wanting you! This is our first chance all day—"

He was about to smother her words with his mouth, when a muffled cry came through the wall.

"What the hell's over there?"

The sound was repeated, accompanied by the sound of breaking crockery.

"It can only be Flo and McConnell!"

Jenny guided Pike's mushroom to her hot, wet folds. The big man cupped her buttocks with his hands, thrust into her.

They pumped and they bucked.

Chapter 5

"Didn't mean to knock over the damned ewer," Skins said. He looked ruefully down at the puddle at his feet, the scattered shards surrounding the wash stand.

"So you were in a big hurry to climb into the hay. No harm done. Just don't go cutting your feet on that busted crockery."

Flo was wearing nothing but a tortoiseshell comb in her long darkish hair. Her wedge of kinky body nap was the same reddish-brown, and fully as resplendent. As she bent from the waist, her rounded breasts swung succulently. The rounded columns of her legs tapered to trim ankles. The pink lips at her crotch pouted.

"You're a real dish, Flo, and that's the truth." But Skins looked askance at her petite frame, imperceptibly wagged his head.

"If you're wondering about my size, I'm big where I gotta be. Here, let me see all of you." She dragged down his drawers, exposing his penis. "You're hung like a horse, but I can handle you. In fact I *want* that hunk of meat. Don't make me wait longer!"

With feline grace she drew Skins by his member, and they flopped down on the mattress. Kissing hungrily, Skins played with her breasts, feeling the nipples grow hard as rifle balls. She threw her arms about him and spread her legs, tipping the mountain man onto his back.

His fingers were at her velvety sex, feeling the cleft's hot wetness. Flo's touch on him became urgent. Smooth legs pressed his sides as she mounted his monster.

A growl of pleasure rose in her throat. He pumped his hardness into her wet, hot tunnel. "Like this?" he rasped.

"Yes! Like that! But harder! Harder!"

In the next room Pike and Jenny, bodies locked, squirmed and thrashed like a couple of beached mackerel. With the big mountain man in the saddle, the woman groaned at each slam of his pubic bone. "Oh!" she cried. "Oh!" She clamped his waist with upraised legs.

She was a heated bitch, a she-cat, unhinged with frenzy. She growled, "Nearly there, Pike! I'm nearly there! Don't stop!"

Stopping was the last thing he—or his cock— wanted. He kept grinding, but not just because she begged him. He was hot for this action, volcano hot and seething.

So mindlessly did he hump this woman, he scarcely heard the racket in the next room.

Flo Lipscomb gripped McConnell's balls and squeezed enticingly. His manhood grew and dove to her womb.

"Give it to me, Skins! Give it to me!"

He found her joy trigger with a finger, and gently caressed the little tab of flesh. She groaned and clawed him with frantic hands. The man's and woman's pelvises ground. Then Flo's body began to shudder. Skins redoubled his thrusts.

The woman's orgasm swept over her in waves that turned to tides, rocking her. Her body tightly locked with his, she thrashed at each spasming climax. Unmindful, the man drilled into her. Delight filled her brimful.

Then came Skins's own climax. He was jolted, as if by lightning, and his seed jetted. Flo squealed and giggled. Limp, he fell away from her.

"Sleep now," he groaned.

Within a minute they both were snoring.

Jack Pike felt his semen boiling. In his ears, he heard: "I want you to come! *I'm* coming! Ah-aa-aah!"

"Yeah!" Pike grunted. "Yeah!" He rode the woman to glory.

She collapsed across him, leaking his fluids. Her

voice was like a kitten's purr: "Oh, yeah, Pike, that was fine. Really fine!"

"Hush." He closed her mouth with a gentle finger.

Sleep found them, wrapped them in its soothing blanket.

Chapter 6

As a feeble winter sun slanted beams through the windows of the stockroom at Fort Graybull, two hard-bitten older men tramped the aisles between the piles of goods—from shooting gear and food staples, to colorful trinkets used in Indian trading. The men's beards were stained with tobacco juice, their faces seamed and weathered under wolverine-fur caps. From their stained and frayed buckskins, they might have been flat broke, but this wasn't the case. The pair was at the post to buy supplies they'd pay for—with credit slips earned from the pelts they'd sold Tim Flanagan.

Tim's paper was as good as gold at his post. This pair of trappers knew that—as did almost every mountain man in the Bitterroots.

That was why so many returned yearly to deal at Graybull.

Today Elijah Rowe and Gap-Tooth Williams needed a wide variety of items to see them through the trapping season. Since riding in shortly after sunup they'd been picking out their selections, and burlap sacks stuffed with these leaned against the counter: gunpowder, firing flints, lead for molding rifle balls. Plus hatchets, knives and traps.

Now the pair stood at the food-staple counter.

"What's the flour sell for?"

"Three dollars the pound."

"Too much."

Elijah elbowed Gap-Tooth. "We may've just rode in, but we ain't donkey-dumb. We pay heavy for grub, ain't nothin' left to spend on gals. And, Jesus, we like gals!"

"Take it or leave it," snapped the clerk.

"Why, you goddamned pipsqueak—"

A gentling hand fell on Gap-Tooth's shoulder. "Easy, old son. Easy."

Williams pivoted, his hand streaking for his skinning knife. But then he recognized the smile of his friend, Jack Pike. "Jack? Yeah, b'gawd, 'tis!" He stamped a foot and slapped Pike's back. "Look who's here, Elijah!"

Rowe smiled around his large tobacco cud. "Howdy, Jack. Hey, does McConnell happen to be at Graybull too? Skins lost him a shootin' bet. Owes me a belt o' fresh squeezings!"

Pike laughed. "Skins is in the taproom, not twenty paces from this spot."

"Then why in hell we standin' here? With th' whiskey near and me so dry, let's stir our stumps!"

Minutes later Pike, McConnell and the newcomers stood at the plank bar, mugs lifted in round–robin toast. Each of the drinkers roared out in turn.

"To the beaver trade!"

"To women, pale-skinned or brown!"

"To Tim Flanagan—fairest trader north of Taos!"

Elijah echoed Gap-Tooth's sentiment: "May the square-shooter go on prospering!"

McConnel drank and set down his mug. "Don't we wish."

The faces of both Skins and Pike went glum.

"Somethin' the matter, boys?" Gap-Tooth rubbed a nose colored by a purple tracery of broken veins. "Somethin' go wrong for old Flan?"

"Somethin' we might help?" Rowe questioned.

"May's well tell the story, Jack," Skins said.

"Yeah. They'll hear it from somebody soon as late."

For the next few minutes Pike spoke rapidly. ". . . LeSage . . . Ornery booshway . . . Wants Flanagan out of the fur business. Ludlow's Bay planned to build a rival trading post—"

"Don't forget the company's brigade—a private army," Skins reminded.

Pike slapped the bar. "Damn! And their plan is to cut all trails to Graybull. Force the free trappers to sell to *them*. With a hundred riflemen, they could make it work. Us free trappers are tough, but the odds have never been this stiff!"

"Christ!" Williams grumbled.

"Jesus!" said Rowe. "After this, my randy pecker seems chicken shit."

Pike grunted. "Oh, this trip you'll get your

chance at a poke. The ax won't fall till spring. *Then's* when we'll be ass-deep in pelts we got to unload, or else. To whoever—at whatever price we can get."

"What's Tim aim to do?" Gap-Tooth said. "And how'd he get hisself in such a mess? Didn't Ludlow's Bay offer to buy him out?"

Skins and Pike stared into their whiskey. Then Pike lifted his eyes to the old-timer's. "I'll tell you what happened. I spoke up for Tim, told LeSage what he could do with his offer. You can guess why, Gap-Tooth. I hate to see Tim go."

Elijah's mouth trickled brown juice. "You only feel the same as us. Most of us old boys have tangled with Ludlow's Bay afore. It's another company out to rook the little guy."

"I'll tell you something," McConnell put in. "Ludlow's prices will be poorer than Tim's. Ludlow's will buy pelts cheap and sell goods high!"

"Christ! How'll the trappers fare then? Why, poorly!" Elijah Rowe was getting fighting mad. His hand slapped the butt of his Lancaster flintlock pistol.

At that moment burly Tim Flanagan burst through the batwings. Scurrying to keep up with the Irishman was Flo, now in a flouncy dress sewn from scarlet cloth. The eyes of Rowe and Williams popped.

Skins signaled the bar dog for refills. Pike stood in silence, wrapped in thought.

Flanagan's voice was boisterous: "Elijah and Gap-Tooth, by Mary and the saints! Heard ye'd ridden in—and knowed what ye'd be wanting. So here's the wench to warm your ashes!"

49

"I'm Flo." The sorrel-head winked. "And I'm available."

Rowe's jaw dropped. "And I'm damned!"

Tim said, "Hurry off with the lady, boyos. I'll just stay behind here, talk to Pike."

The woman let the men size her up. Much of interest showed: a soft throat, upper bosom. Above her scooped neckline, the edges of rouged nipples.

The mountain men were sweating.

Flo led Elijah and Gap-Tooth toward the door, but turned, scampering back to McConnell. "Skins, I hope you understand," she whispered. "I make my living by going to bed with men. I'm getting together a stake, so's next spring I can move to the Oregon country, where I figure a woman can have a future."

Skins shrugged. "A gal's gotta do what a gal's gotta do."

She scampered back to join her johns.

Pike, McConnell and Flanagan adjourned to a table where a bottle waited. The trader clamped his teeth into the cork, jerked it free, and splashed whiskey into mugs for all three.

When Tim spoke, he seemed almost tongue-tied. "Jack and Skins, I done a heap of thinkin' since last night. I've got me chances calc'lated, and they don't look good. I ain't coward nor quitter, but if LeSage builds his new post, I'm lost. Look what Ludlow's Bay did before, all up and down the Missouri River."

Pike recalled, "For a couple years they paid top dollar for furs. But once the other traders got frozen out, Ludlow's Bay dropped prices. The pay was stingy, but free trappers were treed. They had no choice but take what they could get."

"Bad times," Skins summed up. "Real bad."

"So, see how it stands, boyos." Flanagan hauled himself to his feet. He staggered a bit.

Pike noticed, and started talking rapidly. "Hold on, Tim. What you're saying is, you've decided to float, not paddle. So the current seems to be against you. When the waters empty through the busted beaver dam—"

"I'll sink. Sure, and what else can happen? 'Tain't after me to wage a price war. It'd only drag out the ending."

"Down in the mouth, Tim?"

"Aye!"

Pike slapped his back. "Y'know, I been thinking too—but along happier lines. Here's a notion: how about fighting back, winning? You can beat LeSage, with help from friends."

"Friends like you and Skins?"

"And more. Men like Gap-Tooth and Elijah, who're already here at Graybull. Plus Jim Beckwourth and Milt Sublette, who're up in the mountains someplace. If they're close by, they'd want to help. Whiskey Sam Benedict's the type to join—along with all your other longtime customers."

Tim scratched his head. " 'Tis wild, these things ye say—"

"Keep listening." To McConnell, he added, "You too, Skins. Now Tim, we know LeSage is poison—deadly as a timber rattler. And far from stupid, so don't turn your backs. The thing to do is act tough—and go on acting tough."

"With nothin' to back it up? His brigade'll keep the trappers from reachin' Graybull."

"Not a tribe of trappers sworn to you, Tim! Not a Flanagan brigade!"

McConnell before had heard Pike talk like this. He meant what he said. Fact was, he was *willing* things to happen, and when Jack Pike did that, things *did* happen—most of the time.

Skins drank, felt the liquor burn his gullet. Now Pike leaned back, nonchalant.

Skins was damned curious as to what Pike would say next . . .

Chapter 7

Jenny nudged the door to Flo's room open a crack, just enough to take a quick peek inside. She glimpsed the bed and her friend reclining on it, legs outstretched. As she watched, Gap-Tooth Williams put his bald, jug-eared head to the redhead's crotch and started lapping. The eager lip-smacking of the old-timer kept tempo with the twitching of his withered buttocks above his dropped britches. Abandoning his mouth-hold and flopping atop the woman, the veteran mountain man jammed his peg where the sun doesn't shine. The woman's legs lifted as he plunged, pumping for all he was worth.

Without a sound Jenny eased the door shut, heaved a sigh, leaned her back against the scarred adobe wall. She didn't think she'd have much of a wait. If she knew men—which she surely did— Gap-Tooth wouldn't take long.

She drew a tiny file from her britches pocket, began buffing her fingernails.

Inside, the graybeard, starved for wick-dipping after months in the high country, made the most of this hot woman to whom he'd promised a dollar. She'd locked her fingers behind his stringy neck, thrust her face into the hollow of his shoulder. He felt the moistness of her lips tracking down along his chest.

The woman was good—his rod wasn't likely to go off too soon—or worse, go limp. Now she nibbled his ear like a grazing shoat, exploring with her tongue, swirling and lapping, driving him crazy.

Jesus!

As for Flo, she pressed her eyelids shut and gave herself up to the sensations jolting through her. She was quivering from top to toe, her centers of feeling the thumb-sized nipples, the depths of her love tunnel. "Attaway, mister," she encouraged. "I want this! Christ, Gap-Tooth! Yes! Yes!"

Encased his full-length in her, Gap-Tooth picked up his stroking. The swollen plumb-tip of his cock twitched and throbbed. He drove in and out, in and out with the energy of a steam piston.

"Never mind me, Gap," Flo urged him. "Have your own good time. That's what you paid for."

"Bullshit!"

Why, the gent was actually holding back for her sake! To give her the time that she needed, in order to come! When most men were concerned totally with their own pleasure. Now Flo's breaths were whistling in her nostrils, her ripe breasts heaving.

Gap-Tooth felt the woman's shuddering climax, heard the groan of ecstasy rise in her throat: "Yes!

Yes!" Then his stalk still almost stiff, he grunted like a rooting razorback.

He emptied into the woman.

He flopped off her and lay unmoving.

"Gap? You all right?"

He sat bolt-upright on the tick, stretched his arms high, grinned. He crowed, "Ya-*hoo!*"

He was fine—never feeling better.

"Yee-*hah,* hell-for-leather and come Sunday! Hot damn, but ain't I a man and a half?"

"You're still a stud, old-timer."

" 'Scuse me, gal. It's drinkin' time!" He was tugging on his britches, tying up his shirt. "Christ! What a thirst! Oh, here! I 'most forgot." He tossed a shiny dollar, which Flo caught in midair, spinning.

When he'd gathered up the knives and powder horns he'd shed, he paused. "Be seein' ya, gal," he mumbled. He saluted, and then he sauntered out the door.

Jenny, who'd been marking time in the passageway, thrust in her head. "He's a randy old fella."

Flo was buttoning a flannel wrap across her lush breasts. "Gap is surprising for his age. But then, he's a tough mountain man. But say, look!" She showed Jenny her bright dollar. "Jen, you know the reason I service men. My dream of Oregon, it comes closer with every man I take to bed." She hugged herself. "Next westbound pack train, make room for me! Can't hardly wait!"

"You're counting on a new start, come spring?"

"I live for it."

The next thing Jenny said surprised Flo. "Maybe I'll just go along. Avoid the trouble that might be heading Graybull-way."

Jenny didn't smile, and Flo was curious. "You heard something I haven't? Something bad?"

"You know about the Ludlow's Bay men who were here yesterday? Drinking in the taproom, picking fights?"

"Some of them did other things. But go on."

"Well here's what Skins said . . ."

In a few words, she related McConnell's information. That the brigade men, under Baptiste LeSage, would build a Ludlow's Bay outpost close to Graybull. Thus, the company would gain its foothold on the Yellowstone.

"Damn," Flo put in. "Tim Flanagan's a decent sort. What a shame, his days in business being numbered. A big company can afford to take losses at a new post for years, the amounts offset by *other* profits—"

"You get the gist," Jenny said. "Tim's worried as hell. But Pike's cooked up a plan: to get the free trappers to cooperate. LeSage threatens that when the free trappers bring their harvests down, they'll be kept from Graybull. Brigade men will be posted on the trails, and they'll try to persuade the mountain men to deal at new Fort Ludlow. If they won't agree, LeSage's men will kill 'em and take their pelts."

"Free trappers are no pushovers—"

"But each, by himself, will be outnumbered. Plus, they won't be their best to fight, with loaded packhorses to tend, being low on gunpowder at end of season." Jenny began to pace. "So Pike wants to let the free trappers know—now. He wants to send McConnell, Williams and Rowe out. They'll urge trappers to team up, just for this winter. All cooperate, work Eagle Valley, the best beaver grounds left in the mountains. The system would work like a brigade—but the men wouldn't be company men. At season's end, each catch belongs to one owner."

Flo puzzled. "There'd still be the problem of getting to Graybull."

"But don't you see?" Jenny stopped pacing, planted a foot atop a scuffed, brass-bound chest on the floor. "Pike's band would come out in a bunch! That way they could fight their way to Graybull, sell their furs to Flanagan, break the blockade!"

Flo whistled. "McConnell told you this?"

"Just now."

"Sounds like a good idea. Give your man— Pike—credit!"

Jenny shrugged. "I know how tough Pike is, and how savvy. He's earned the Indian name He-Whose-Head-Touches-the-Sky. Tim Flanagan told me. But as for him being my man—"

Flo had crossed to the chest and crouched down, the silver coin still between her fingers. "In a minute we'll talk about plans, Jen, but now I got to stash this dollar. Move your foot?"

When she opened the lid, hinges protested. But those squawkings were drowned out by the woman's wail of surprise. "The hell! What son of a bitch—?"

She was rummaging frantically, elbow-deep in the women's clothes in the chest.

"What's wrong?" said Jenny.

"What's wrong? My poke's gone! Buckskin pouch with the hundred dollars I saved!" Flo was mad as a cat, and her eyes blazed. But tears rolled down her cheeks, as well.

"All my money! My Oregon stake! Gone!"

"Lordy!"

"Oh, but I'll get it back, Jenny!" Flo blurted. "By Christ, I'll get it back! The john that took it, it had to've been that frog yesterday! Louis Charbeau! Oh, won't I go after him!"

Her next words were a low hiss. "Do this, and it's get-even time! I'll bring the bastard's balls back with me! I swear it!"

Chapter 8

Jack Pike stood in the central compound of the Fort Graybull post, amid large and small piles of supplies, from flour and coffee by the gunnysackful to small kegs of gunpowder, bars of Galena lead. And hand-forged beaver traps—hundreds of traps. Overhead the early-winter sky hung low and glowering, but it didn't appear ready to snow. That was why Pike and the others worked so hard, sweat dampening their wind-chapped faces. Although conditions weren't pleasant outside, they'd be getting worse. A lot worse, once winter settled in with a vengeance.

Out of the adobe housing the taproom, Skins McConnell strolled jauntily. "Making headway, Jack?"

"Tolerable. Look for yourself." Pike made a sweeping gesture.

A clerk staggered out of a storehouse, across his shoulders a thick bale of wool blankets. He was followed by two more of Tim Flanagan's men, each of whom lugged armloads of axes, hatchets, hammers and more traps. The three men dropped their loads.

Skins's eyes lifted to the mid-distance, spotting Elijah and Gap-Tooth approaching. The mountain men led three horses, rugged mountain-bred animals, saddled for hard mountain trailing. "Ah, here they come. Elijah and Gap, ready to ride out."

"That a new badger cap, Skins?" Pike asked.

"Yeah, and a warm one." Skins's hand went to the silky fur. "Anything to stay warm. No willing women where me and the boys are heading."

"You figured your route?"

Skins bobbed his chin. "Me, I'll make tracks for Summit Pass. Elijah's bound for Gros Ventra. Gap-Tooth drew the short straw, and'll be riding north to the Piney Slopes."

The men stood with the horses. "Fellas," Pike said, "you look fit to wrestle grizzlies. But you know what you really need to do."

Gap-Tooth grinned gap-toothedly. "Sure. Tell every coon we see 'bout your plan for Eagle Valley. Say that Jack Pike, hisself, is organizin' the camp, gatherin' supplies, and'll meet 'em there. That the valley's rich, plenty of furs for all. And that they, too, oughtta pass the word to others they meet!"

The mountain man squinted. "Er . . . ya *do* aim to be there afore us, Jack?"

Pike pointed. Across the yard, a band of Indians—fifteen braves, plus women and children—

60

stood against the far palisade. Some lounged, others worked at packing quill-worked parfleches. They had their own riding ponies. "Sure, I'll be at Eagle Valley first—with the help of my Snake tribe friends. And with a full-loaded pack train." Pike went on to assure, "If I didn't mean business, I wouldn't have hired the redskins."

Rowe spoke up. "Your plan's a good one, Jack. If you roped me in, it's got to be. I never work with pards, but this time it makes sense to. Ludlow's Bay Company's gotta be headed off. They're out to skin our asses."

"They *will* be headed off."

"Well, time to ride," said Williams. He stepped into his mount's stirrup, swung stiffly aboard. The collar of his blanket coat was up. A rolled buffalo robe was tied behind his cantle.

Elijah Rowe swung into the saddle. His animal crow-hopped a bit. It had been picked for sure-footedness, not sweet temper.

"You fellas ride on ahead," McConnell directed. "I'll catch up." As they moved from earshot, he told Pike, "Hope a good crew gathers in that valley. What Gap-Tooth said was right." He slung his rifle over his shoulder by a whang cord. "Mountain men can rub each other wrong. Why, at one rendezvous, there were so many brawls—"

"I figure I can handle the men."

Skins sized up Pike as he had many times, and came to the same conclusion. Here was a six-foot-four, two-hundred-forty pound giant. His arms were stout as branches, legs like pillars of stone. And Pike was quick as a wildcat, despite his size.

The man's shooting skills were legendary, and was known to have killed a grizzly bare-handed.

He would be able to handle almost anything.

"We're counting on you, He-Whose-Head-Touches-the-Sky."

Skins added, "I'm hoping you don't lose any of those Snake females." He nodded at the Indians, in their warm garb of doubled buckskin. "Most are damned good-looking. See the one with apple breasts? She's giving us the eye."

"Been looking at us both, you say?"

"You bet!"

"Are we both gonna have her at the same time, or will you go first, or me go first?" Pike wore a huge grin and laughed.

"Oh shit, Jack. I reckon we can divvy later. You know me, though—always thinking of women flesh. Too bad Flo and Jenny want to stay behind."

"They're better off at Graybull, Skins. You know it. Being from back east, they're not used to mountain hardship. The cold, the loneliness—"

"But they *wouldn't* be lonely, with us! Nor would we be lonely! We'd all keep company!"

Whenever his friend got to talking orgies, Pike figured it was time to change the subject. "Well," he said, "seeing how neither gal shows interest, we have to accept it. By the way, Skins, oughtn't *you* show an interest? In riding out? Elijah and Gap are nearly to the foothills."

McConnell turned and looked. "By god, you're right."

He leaped into the saddle. "See you in a few weeks, Jack!"

He kicked the horse's sides, and the chestnut moved out. Once he was through the gate, Skins lifted his mount to a lope. It was clear he'd overtake the others.

By the time Skins, Rowe and Williams were specks against the mountains' vastness, Pike turned to the clerks. "Get this stuff packed! Me and the Snakes move out at sunup with the pack train!"

"Yessir!"

"Oh, Mr. Pike? Yonder comes Miss Henderson walking."

Jenny had emerged from an adobe and strode up to Pike. A soft breast brushed his arm. " 'Lo, Pike. Got a minute?"

"Pretty busy just now, Jenny." The towheaded kid was making a botch of packing foodstuffs. Pike itched to teach him the diamond hitch.

"I'm not flirting, Pike. This is about Flo."

Pike guided the woman to a wall that broke the wind.

"What's wrong, Jenny?"

"Like I said, it's Flo. She's gone off on foot, more than two hours ago. Just walked out the back gate. When she didn't come back, I started to worry."

Pike scowled. "Why'd she pull that damn-fool stunt?"

"She had a reason. Somebody stole her cash stash! All the money she'd accumulated!"

Pike waited for more, and Jenny continued. "Flo trusts everyone at Graybull, Flanagan's people. Is certain they'd never rob her. But there was a certain stranger at the post yesterday, one of the brigade crowd. Called himself Louis Charbeau.

63

He wanted a turn in the sack, she took him to her room. Left him alone a minute while she went for whiskey."

"Are you saying—?"

Jenny's eyes grew huge. "Oh, Pike. Flo did want her money back! And to get it, she hiked to LeSage's camp!"

Chapter 9

"Louis Charbeau! I want to see Louis Charbeau!"

"L-lady, you dunno what you're asking—"

Flo shook her mane of flaming hair, let fall open her bulky blanket coat, exposing pink skin of upper breasts above her blouse. During the walk to the edge of the brigade's camp, her anger had grown. Now she sensed she'd get nowhere unless she hid it. "I'm a fancy lady, staying at Graybull. Me and Louis—bless his heart—well, yesterday we . . . well, *you* know!" She dropped the sentry a sexy wink.

He looked to be green and slow witted. His jaw was slack, his eyes were crossed. Canting his rifle at the sky, he resumed stuttering, "L-like I s-said, I ain't supposed to—" Then his unfocused gaze took in the cloud of hair, the red lips, the come-hither look. The young man's mouth-corners turned up. "Oh, I g-get it: ye be a whore. Any chance I might get up yer skirts?"

"Likely, big boy. Why not? But first I got to give Louis something he forgot last time. Won't take long. Which tent is his?"

"Down that street, toward th' far end."

Flo followed the pointing finger. Behind her she heard: "Don't g-go forgettin' Li'l Carl! Li'l Carl, that's me!"

The path was puddled, which was strange, since there'd been no rain for days. The tents resembled those in an army camp, with ropes snubbed tight and canvases taut.

Now in late-afternoon light, the men lounged about. A few smoked short-stemmed clay pipes, others gambled, either with bone dice or tattered cards. All the brigade men's faces appeared criminal-like: scars and crooked noses abounded. So did missing teeth, lost ears and lost fingers.

Their buckskins were filthy, and as Flo walked, her nose picked up a stench. The puddles, she realized, brimmed with urine. Catcalls began to fill the air: "What tits! *Mon Dieu!*"

"*Mademoiselle!* Give me your cunt!"

"No, *my* cock's biggest! Try me!"

Flo kept striding, looking neither left nor right. Abruptly a bush-bearded man with a deerskin eye patch stepped into her path. He wasn't going to allow her past. His slit mouth was ugly and twisted.

With rage? With lust?

"What the woman wanting in LeSage's camp? You tell Jules Mercier—that's me!" He put a fist to his chest. "Or do I got to force you?"

Used to dealing with his type, she stood her ground. "I'm Flo Lipscomb," she announced, "and I'm here on an errand. An important errand." In-

66

side her coat pocket one hand clutched a horse pistol, the other a butcher knife. Her mind was solely on her mission. She wouldn't be selling herself today. She doubted these scoundrels would pay her.

She tried a smile. "Jules. Nice name. Pleased to meet you, Jules. Listen, I'm looking for Louis Charbeau." She moved her hand to indicate his height. "Long-drink-of-water build, maybe six feet? Moustache, squinty eyes? A real generous gent, for a Frenchy."

Mercier sputtered an oath: "*Sacrebleu*! *I* too am French-Canadian! From Montreal!"

"You're a long way from home! But getting back to Louis—"

"Who's looking for me? I'm coming!" The man who'd bought Flo's services the day before ran up. He'd rushed from a tent with his shirttails flapping. His face showed pure contempt. His hammer-hard fists were bunched.

"It's me. Flo." Now to get him to a place where they'd be alone . . .

"The whore Flo? Why you come to camp? This?" He drew out her draw-stringed poke, jingled it. As he taunted her, guffaws rang out—sinister guffaws.

"W-well, maybe I was a mite rash—"

"Wait!" He blocked her retreat. "You ain't goin' noplace! Head her off, *mes amis!* We'll teach her a lesson."

She showed the pistol she'd brought, thumbed the hammer back. "Take a step, I'll shoot!"

"Haw!" Charbeau slapped the firearm aside. "Has she more weapons? Grab her! What? A toad stabber?"

The man's heel dealt a blow to Flo's backside, sending her sprawling. She was being held on the ground by strong hands. "Stop! You can't do this!"

She tried to sit up, and her upper body was seized, pressed back. Her wrists were grabbed, and so was her hair. Brawny Louis Charbeau stood over her, mouth twisted, cap pushed back. Flo attempted a kick, but her ankles were pressed to the earth.

"Now, *mademoiselle*—"

"Bastard!"

The man bent down, dug his fingers into the neck of her clothing, tearing. Like peeling a corn ear. Soon chilly air raised goosebumps on bare flesh.

Her terrified eyes saw lewdly grinning men line up. The first of the lot—Charbeau—dropped his britches.

His exposed lance was stiffly erect, odoriferous.

Chapter 10

"LeSage's camp?" Pike blurted to Jenny, amazed. "Flo went to LeSage's camp?" The clerks in the yard of Fort Graybull stood and stared at the couple. Several loafing Snake Indians showed curiosity, too.

"Like I told you, Pike, she went after that bastard who screwed her, Charbeau. If you aim to fetch her out of that hot seat, I'll keep you company."

"Oh, *I'm* on my way, all right, but you're staying right here. Where you'll be safe. Got it?"

Jenny faltered, overpowered by Pike's will. "I hear what you're saying, Pike. I'll wait at the post with Flanagan."

The mountain man nodded curtly, then turned and picked up his Hawken from where he'd rested it against a wall. Next he marched to the saddled horse waiting at the hitch rail. Pike's brain raced. Standing beside the mount he meant to borrow, he uncapped the smaller of his two powder horns, primed the rifle afresh, and then his Kentucky pistol. To the chief clerk he barked, "Tell your boss I've ridden over to LeSage's camp. Jenny knows the details, and can tell him the reason."

"Awright, Pike. Good luck, goin' agin that tribe o' polecats."

He swung into the saddle, and as he trotted toward the back gate, Pike loosened his knife's blade in its sheath at his belt. Once out and onto the flat, he had no trouble picking up Flo's tracks. They were dark smudges on the frosty ground, and led off north across a series of bare hills.

Lesage's camp was a bad destination for anyone who wanted to stay healthy. The Lipscomb woman's route could lead her to death, or worse.

Unless Pike reached her in time.

"Haw! Plug her, Henri! Do fer th' bitch!"

"Jes' leave some for me! I don' mind a sloppy tenth turn—or so."

The heavy brigade man atop Flo on the ground pumped into her. The more hurt he could inflict on the helpless woman, the more he liked it. Spending in a flood, he rolled to his feet, then kicked her brutally in the short ribs.

Flo stifled a cry. Crying only seemed to make things worse. For almost an hour now, pain filled all parts of her, but the queue of men stayed about as long, as the brutes who'd used her lined up for more turns.

Her thighs were bruised blue.

Crimson blood leaked between them.

Her punished vagina felt as if on fire. By now

70

she'd been raped so many times, she'd lost count—this after the eighth or ninth brigade man had rammed in his engorged member. Would the brutes ever grow weary? And if the agony and humiliation *did* cease . . . then what? Would they kill her?

By now, Flo accepted the closeness of death.

She opened her eyes to see a silhouetted figure: yet another man. She shuddered, wished she could faint. It was the ugly, scar-faced LeSage, the front of his trousers bulging. He'd already taken her twice, and was back for more.

She'd have preferred any of the others. This particular man was evil incarnate. Aside from his hideous appearance, he delighted in inflicting pain, *lived* to inflict it. Now he crouched at the woman's feet, the empty right eye socket forming a snake's-mouth slit. Brown teeth showed in a malicious grin.

Oh, God, Flo thought. Not again. *Please!*

But his lone cruel eye raked the naked, cringing woman. "Now I gonna let you spread your legs," he rasped, "for a real stud. I goin' to love doin' it to you. You might as well like it, too. LeSage, he's a better *homme* than any other, no? Say it!"

LeSage dropped his britches. His short, fat penis, fully erect, wagged like a puppy's tail. Then the man knelt, pressed Flo down strongly, put his sausage to her portal. She shuddered, loathing the man.

"Take this!" he hissed.

He thrust himself.

Flo held back a scream as LeSage's dry, abrasive member lanced her. She twisted like a hooked fish. The agony was piercing.

To keep from going mad, her mind banished the present. She fought to recall the good times. Some of the best had been spent with Skins McConnell.

"Oh, McConnell! Why can't *you* be here?"

"*Merci,* bitch!" LeSage withdrew from her abused body and jumped up. He planted his heel in the middle of her face, bore down like a miller grinding corn. Fifty brigade men crowded and cheered.

"Attaway, boss!"

"Don't let her talk back!"

"*Mais non!* Punish her!"

LeSage peered around. "Charbeau," he roared. "I'm through with her, this one can be carved. You may do the honors!"

Louis stepped forward. Behind the fearsome black mustachios, he glowered. In his hand was an iron-bladed tomahawk.

He grabbed Flo's brown-tipped breast, pressed with his weapon. There was much craning of brigade men's necks. Everyone wanted a good view.

But just then, hoofbeats sounded through the camp. A rider urged a galloping horse among the tents. As the mount bore down, a shot boomed out. Charbeau screamed and dropped his tomahawk, his face became a sheet of blood. His nose had been blown away, and chalky cheekbone flashed. The dying man performed a back flip.

Pike, his rifle discharged, now drew his pistol. Aimed at LeSage. At the touch of the rein, the horse reared on hind legs.

"Pike!" Flo warned. "Behind you!"

The threatening bush-loper held a hand cannon. The weapon pointed upward at Pike, its range less than three feet. As the big man watched, his foe squeezed the trigger.

Jack Pike looked death in the face.

It would be rocketing toward him, with a pistol ball's speed!

Chapter 11

Sparks showered from the pistol's flint, and a hissing fizzle in the foe's priming pan! The misfire saved Jack Pike's life! But the big man didn't rest on luck. In return, he triggered his handgun, the report banged, the ball drilled Claude Renaud's throat. The wound was fatal, and the man fell, but his companions' guns blazed on all sides. Hot lead whizzed past Pike as he jumped from the saddle. He dashed toward Flo, still on her back, buck naked and blood-caked.

"Mes amis!" came a shout. "Look who's here! The giant from Fort Graybull!"

"Oui!" My knife blade's for his guts!"

"Knife? *Sacrebleu!* Cave his head with a hatchet!"

A jasper blocked Pike's path, and he closed with him, parrying a knife swoop with his forearm. A fringe was clipped from Pike's sleeve. "Flo," he snapped. "Up off your ass! Run for my horse!"

From the corner of his eye, he glimpsed a blond-bearded fellow edging for a clear shot. He slashed at his attacker, opening the chest from nipple to navel.

A heavy .60 caliber pellet missed its target, slammed a Canadian. Pike grabbed the dead man's hand ax. As a horseman trotted up, the big man hurled the tool. The horse's nose was split and blood gushed forth, drenching him.

The animal dropped atop its rider, whose chest was crushed. *"Mon Dieu!* I die! The pain!"

Meanwhile, Pike, helping Flo, was closed in on. His roundhouse punch cracked Bart Seagram's jaw, and the Ludlow's Bay man reeled off, howling.

Another enemy pointed a newfangled cap-and-ball rifle. Panicked Ike Jenks triggered hastily. The rifle ball nipped a hole in Pike's trouser seam. Pike roared his version of a Cheyenne war whoop, and lunged. Jenks's pig eyes bulged in desperation, he reversed his gun in his grip, swung it.

Jenks didn't hear the sound, as Flo Lipscomb cocked the pistol she'd scooped up. Nor the fire-arm's ear-splitting *bam*. But the man was knocked down when a half-ounce slug slammed his belly. Pressure from within pushed out sausages of gut, which bulged through helpless fingers.

He went down, eyes glazing as he screamed.

Pike bit out, "Obliged, Flo! Now take my hand! Let's go!"

The big man and the naked beauty sprinted. Pike leaped to his mount's back, then dragged her up behind, urging the animal to run. The gelding shot off, sure-footed even on frozen turf.

Flo glanced over her shapely shoulder. Over the

hoof-drumming she called out, "Nobody's chasing us!"

"Not yet," Pike snapped. "It'll take time to saddle horses, get weapons reloaded. We're lucky." He slowed the bay to a walk, shrugged out of his jacket and draped the woman to cover her goose-bumped nakedness. "There," he grunted. "That warm you some?"

"Yes, thank you." She fixed the mountain man with a grateful look. "Pike, they put me through real hell. Then you showed up. I can't believe you took on the whole camp. Oh, I've heard the stories—about Jack Pike being king of the mountains. Damned if they aren't true!"

"Glad to've been able to save you, Flo. But now I've got our next move to figure out." He gave the horse its head, knowing it would trot toward home. "Our getaway's got to rile LeSage plenty. But he's not the kind to ignore company orders. He wasn't sent out here to butcher women. Let me think a spell."

They rode without talk; then as the bay topped a rise, they saw a half-dozen riders loping their way. Pike chose not to flee.

"Who are *they?*" Flo questioned.

"Friends!"

In a few minutes they closed with the party. Pike reined up in their midst, a choking cloud of dust rising. It was Flanagan's bunch, including Tim, Jenny and four clerks, all armed and ready for trouble. "I know ye said to wait at Graybull," Tim blurted, "but—"

Pike glanced at Jenny, who forked a skittish pinto. "True, I like my orders followed—most

76

times. But now, it happens I'm glad to see you. LeSage and his outfit'll be on our heels."

Flanagan swore. "Christ!"

"I don't want 'em riding to your post," Pike stated flatly. "So here's what I aim to do. Listen!"

In a few words, Pike outlined his plan. "Me, Jenny and Flo, each on our own horse, will hightail. Losing ourselves will be easy in the foothills. LeSage has got trackers, but those lands, I know 'em like my paw's old back forty."

Flanagan scratched his ear. "Won't LeSage send boys to me tradin' post?"

"Doubtful," Pike opined. "*Me and Flo* are the ones he's pissed at. And being a company man, he's got his orders. He'll be leery of overstepping his authority. Marauding Graybull would be a serious overstep. And if Flo and I aren't there to get even with—"

"Makes sense," Flanagan said.

Jenny pointed across the flat. "Here they come!"

"Flo, let one of Flanagan's men give you his horse! Climb aboard pronto."

While Flo hurriedly swapped mounts, Pike rode a short way off with Tim. Pike asked a question he knew the answer to. "You know Black Feather, the Snake subchief—"

"Leader of the band you hired?"

"That's him. Tim, you've got to carry him a message."

"Aye. And that I'll do!"

"The pack train with all those supplies I bought for wintering. The chief should move the horses out at daybreak. Tell Black Feather I'll meet him three days from now, up at Slippery Rock Lake. It's a hard place to find, but he knows the mountains and he knows Slippery Rock. From the lake we'll all trail together to Eagle Valley."

Flanagan grinned. "So the plan for free trappers to cooperate for a season—'tis still on?"

Pike's arm ached and throbbed from his bullet crease, but he grabbed Tim's hand and pumped. "Sure, it's on. Jack Pike doesn't go back on his word."

"Yer a helluva man, Jack!"

Pike looked at Flo, whose bruised face reflected her fatigue. She needed to be told the truth. "We're in for a ride," the big man said to her. "A hard ride. Neither you or your friend Jenny belong in these parts now. Not after what happened. You're coming with me."

"Both of us? Up into the mountains?"

"Clear to Eagle Valley."

The women exchanged glances between them. "Thanks, Pike," said Flo.

Jenny seconded her. "I'm grateful, too, for what you're doing, Pike."

The big man flicked the reins on his mount's neck. "Let's get a move on." He kicked his horse into a gallop, and the women urged their mounts forward. Soon they settled into a mile-eating pace that could be maintained for hours.

To the west, the high peaks brushed the sky, snowcapped, awesome.

Chapter 12

Night shrouded the foothills, and the bone-wracking chill did its best to make Pike, Jenny and Flo miserable. Fortunately, riding into this godforsaken country both the women's horses had carried spare bedding blankets. As camp was being made in the bottom of a ravine, the women bundled themselves in the warm five-pointers. Pike kept warm by work: stripping the saddles from the mounts and laying out bedrolls under a rock-shelf overhang. There'd been an Indian parfleche behind the saddle of the bay, and the contents—pemmican—would make the threesome an unheated supper.

"Can we have coffee with the eats?" Jenny asked.

"We've got no coffee beans," Pike responded.

"Then a fire? So we can get warm?"

"I'd as soon not take that risk," the big man said. "Smoke can be smelled by enemies. Some of Le-

Sage's men are Huron half-breeds, and there's some smart noses in the bunch." The women sat on the stony ground, legs curled under them. Pike, hunkering, doled out handfuls of greasy, strong-smelling food. "Eat up, gals."

Flo swallowed a morsel, didn't complain. Jenny, on the other hand, wondered alone. "Pike, what the hell *is* this stuff?"

"Like I told you, pemmican is Indian-made food, fit for when a body's on the trail and can't cook. The squaws chop up deer meat, mix in mashed roots and berries, and let the mess dry in the sun. As the final touch, buffalo fat gets added. And I won't lie to you—it's aged."

Jenny's mouth puckered. "Aged? Half spoiled, don't you mean?"

"It's filling and nourishing," Pike said, munching. Then, noticing how quiet Flo had grown, he asked her, "Your belly tolerating it, gal?"

A nod.

"How you feeling? I mean, what with the damage after what you've been through?"

Flo's chin sank lower, but her eyes flashed. "I'm bruised from top to toe, and my crotch burns like a candle flame. Tired? I've never felt so tired. Damn it! Damn Louis Charbeau for stealing my money! But I guess I was a silly goose, going after it the way I did."

Not long after, Pike noticed Flo nod off, the moonlight bathing her upturned face. Dressed in clothes lent by Jenny—which didn't fit too well—the rescued woman still looked mighty pretty. Pike tucked her blanket more snugly around her.

From behind him Jenny said, "Beside Flo's blanket, there's one more, not counting the horse blankets."

"Want to share?"

"You bet! Climb out of those damned buckskin pants, join me under the covers!"

And when he dove under with her, he found himself as warm as toast. The heat of Jenny's desire engulfed Jack Pike. He felt the press of her soft breasts, tight belly, silky thighs glued the length of him. She offered her lips in a prolonged kiss, her tongue probing and twining his tongue. Meanwhile, her hand trailed downward to his groin.

He responded to the erotic kneading. As his erection grew, the knob of it became huge and mushroom-round. He decided to take a turn at pleasuring the woman. Thrusting two fingers deep into her slick love canal, he found her love tab and began a tantalizing circular motion.

"Oh, Pike! Pike—O-oh! Oh-h-h!"

Her fingers toyed with his organ, tickled the silk-smooth hood, caressed its hairy length. Pike swung his heavy body over her, let her guide his tip to her puffy folds.

With a low groan, Pike shoved his cock deeply inside Jenny. The woman thrust back at him eagerly.

Buried in wet softness, Pike began to pump, and the woman clasped him with her legs. She sighed, "Make it last! No, bring me off now! Oh, Pike! I want . . . I *need* all this!" As her love-tension built, she began to thrash from side to side.

Beneath him, he felt her shudder, convulse. He

kept pounding with swift lunges, not slowing until the strong spasms no longer racked her. Now, with measured, controlled rhythms, Pike worked his stiff, stout stalk. Finally his own tremors took him, and he released with a hosing gush.

"Oh Pike," the woman sighed as he withdrew and flopped beside her. The pair lay unmoving for a time, and then Jenny suddenly stiffened in his arms. "Flo," she blurted. "For a few minutes there, I forgot all about her. How is she?"

Pike glanced across at the other bedroll. "Well, what we did, Jenny, it doesn't seem to have wakened the gal. Tuckered as she is, she slept right through." He dipped his face, nibbled Jenny's nipple playfully. "By the way, don't you need rest, too?"

But Jenny had already slipped into a deep slumber.

Unable to doze himself, he lay for a long time just looking up at the stars.

A quarter mile away, beyond a ridge topped by a few stunted trees, fifteen riders wearing Canadian-style fur capotes reined their horses in. Baptiste LeSage, who miles back had relinquished lead, trotted his mount forward from the bunch. He snapped out low words to the tracker. "Marcel? How you doing? Don't you find the hoofprints?"

The half-breed smoothed his fur cap. "No, booshway—not on this ground, the kind we been coverin' for miles. It's all shale. For a long way in all directions, nothing but hard shale."

"*Merde!*"

82

LeSage's mount, weary and bad-tempered, tossed its blaze-faced head. But the man allowed himself no more outbursts. The disfigured features went blank as a mask. Calmly the man scanned the surrounding moonlit area, mostly eroded hillsides separated by wide gullies, vegetation sparse. "Pike and those women, they're up here, someplace. They've got to be. Maybe bedded down not far from where we stand. Following 'em from Graybull, we only lost their trail a few miles back."

Marcel Bear shrugged. "Pike is a mountain man's mountain man. That's his reputation. If he came this way, he came on purpose, to give us the slip."

"Their trail's lost, then? No chance of picking it up?"

"No chance. They're gone. Vamoosed."

The wheels in LeSage's brain ground like millstones. What, exactly, was his position? He was his expedition's leader, for one thing, his employer the mighty Ludlow's Bay Fur Company.

And as he was well paid, it was his duty to follow orders.

His first orders had been to try and buy out Tim Flanagan—and there he'd failed. The next step was to build a new trading post. This his men would accomplish during the winter months. By spring the new Fort Ludlow would be open for business.

Ready to buy furs, ready to pay top dollar. Freeze Flanagan out, make the free trappers beholden to the company. And the year following, all competition gone, prices would be forced down.

And Baptiste LeSage, the man in charge, would reap certain promised bonuses . . .

His thoughts were broken in on by Marcel. "What you say, booshway? Turn back?"

Baptiste's lone bloodshot eye blinked. Failure to catch up with Pike? He hated the thought. The mountain man had invaded his camp, rescued the doxy, killed men . . .

And yet . . .

By now, more of his troop had ridden up. Clouding vapor burst from the horses' nostrils. The men heard: "*Oui*, Marcel, now we'll turn back! That's all we can do, *non*? Well, we'll nab Pike in the spring, that's all. He's a free trapper, isn't he? Isn't spring the time we put all free trappers under our thumbs?"

LeSage's second-in-command, Mike Forester, piped up. "Three cheers for Ludlow's Bay Company, and our booshway! Hip-hip—"

"Hooray!" the rest of the gang roared.

"Hip-hip—"

"Hoo-*ray!*"

"Hip-hip—"

"*Hoo*-RAY!"

The voices echoed through the canyon. The men wheeled their horses about, walked them back downslope.

The night again was quiet.

The loudest sound was the thud of LeSage's heart in his chest. He could control his appearance of cool, but the rage was there, inside. But he would have his revenge someday!

"Beware, Jack Pike! Beware," he hissed under his breath.

"Ya say something, booshway?"

LeSage raised his silver-mounted brandy flask.

He swigged deeply. "What I said was, let's ride! We got a trading post to build!"

In a pinyon's high branches, an owl hooted.

Pike stirred next to Jenny's form. Was it a noise he'd heard? A sound like cheering? Out here, hundreds of miles from civilization?

Nuts!

The big man rolled on his side, his eyelids anvil-heavy.

Soon he, too, snored softly in the darkness.

Part Two
The Valley

Chapter 13

Riding through a high, rocky notch flanked by snowcapped mountains, Skins McConnell and a horseman companion sat their saddles easily, sucking breaths of the thin, cold air of early winter in the high country. The men's collars pulled up, their hats tugged low, they looked down on a timberlined natural bowl in the heart of the Bitterroots. Across Eagle Valley gusted a stiff west wind that sent brown leaves in rustling whirls around the horses' legs. Against the background of rugged slopes the valley was beautiful: wooded with birches, aspens, poplars, by now red-leaved or already completely shed. The valley was crisscrossed by streams, most of which had been dammed by beavers.

But the amazing thing to Skins lay at the nearest end. This was a newly thrown-up brigade-type encampment, complete with a variety of lean-to shelters and sheds. There was even one structure that might be called a cabin, having log walls and a steep pole roof.

A small village of Indian lodges lay beyond.

Pike and a number of other trappers had apparently arrived long enough ago to bring things along this far. The community looked well established, if still abuilding. Smoke spiraled lazily from more than a dozen cook fires.

McConnell glanced at his companion, Rufus Brumley, a whiskered bear of a young man, who sat his horse cockily. "Well, Skins, you were right, I got to admit. This place, it sure does 'pear to be a good place. I already see a fine passel of beaver ponds."

It was true; even from up here the miniature lakes could be seen, each containing from two to five dome-shaped stick lodges that reared from the waters.

McConnell noted the angle of the sun. "Ought to be grub on somebody's fire about this time of day. Leastwise, it feels to me near meal time. Like I ain't eaten a hot meal in a week. Let's ride on down."

Clapping heels to their mounts' sides, they guided the horses along the trail down the hillside. Rufus regaled Skins on his good luck, how thankful he was he'd run into Skins, who'd told of this year's trapping camp in Eagle Valley. The place was one of the best grounds left for trappers. As they rode, they followed a gurgling stream, coming to and passing a patch of gnawed-off stumps along the bank. There were several beaver lodges of mud-daubed sticks in the pond, and brown, fat beavers sunned themselves atop them. More of the furry

90

creatures, swimming, made long, rippling wakes on the water's surface.

A flat-sounding *smack* came when a flat tail beat the water. "Looka there!" Rufus pointed. The swimming beavers dived, leaving ripples that bubbled and spread. " 'Pears to be a good-'nuff bunch of living quarters your pard's laid out. But does Pike reckon our bunch'll be able to get to Graybull with our plews, come spring? Them Ludlow's Bay jaspers won't be able to bottle us up?"

McConnell assured the other trapper. "Well, yeah. The way it'll be, LeSage and his boys won't be expecting all the free trappers to ride down from the beaver grounds together. A hard-fighting, fast-shooting bunch." He spat; the wad, when it hit the ground, created an instant thawed spot. "We'll get to Flanagan's, right enough. Just like we'll get to Jack's valley headquarters shack in another minute."

They were riding the last few yards down the path between the newly laid-out campsites. Men of varying appearances—some small of stature, others giants; some blond-bearded, others dark-bearded—showed themselves at the doorways. Jumping the gun on winter, many wore capotes—cloaks—of bearskin or wolfskin. Grins crossed faces, and greetings were shouted. As far as an observer could tell, everyone was friendly.

But then, the long season of beaver trapping had hardly begun.

In years past, McConnell, like most trappers, had spent months away from towns amid trackless mountain wastes, snowed in by twenty-foot drifts, menaced by the possibility of starvation, attacks by beasts, and the other dangers dished up by the wilderness. He knew that if a man was alone, cabin fever could sear his soul and drive him to the point of madness. But if a number of men were forced to live in proximity while isolated, none able to go his own way if inclined, worse things could happen. While a blizzard raged outside, friends could become enemies, fights could break out, knives be slid between the ribs of a cabin-mate.

So what was in store for these strong, independent-minded mountain men in the months ahead?

McConnell's thoughts were broken in on by Rufus. "Thought ya said there wouldn't be no white women up here," Rufus rasped.

"The plan don't call for none, no. The only females up here, supposed to be the Snake squaws. Like their men, brought to help out. Of course, the women's pussy'll be available. Catch a redskin gal's fancy, she'll most times want to try out a fella. And some of 'em are damned *fine* on a soft fur bed—"

"Them two there ain't redskins," Rufus pointed out. McConnell looked that way.

His jaw dropped.

The woman Brumley pointed at was Flo. And she was standing outside the one cabin, with its walls of unpeeled logs and sod. Next to her Jenny Henderson stood. Both the women looked healthy as could be, from the good air. And even at this distance, Skin felt the jolt of the women's sexuality, as his groin started to crawl.

"I'll be damned. There *are* white women, at least two of the sweet critters!" Skins wiped a gloved hand across his face. "Which means, Pike must have changed his plan. Fact is, Rufus, I've met those gals before. Want to bet that's Pike's cabin they're standing in front of?"

By now the women had spotted McConnell. "Skins!" Jenny called, jumping around and waving. Flo acted quieter than her friend, staring at McConnell as if she'd never expected to see him again.

Suddenly the elkhide door flap was thrown back, and Jack Pike emerged, all smiles. "Howdy, Skins, old friend." He gave Rufus a wave also. "Take a load off those horses' backs, fellas. Supper's almost ready."

"Eats! About the onliest thing this coon wants just now!"

McConnell chuckled at Rufus's words, at the same time dismounting. Hands got shaken all around, and the horses were stripped of saddles and packs, hobbled and left to crop grass. Then the whole group trooped inside.

"Food," Skins muttered on the way. "And real, live hostesses!"

Chapter 14

The fire on the crude stone fireplace of the log structure was small, mere. yellow licks of flame sprouting from the red bed of coals. A copper kettle balanced over the heat, and from the pungent, delicious aroma, a rich bear stew was simmered to delicious doneness. The women ladled out bowls of the spicy, thick stuff, then passed them around to the men.

Pike, McConnell and Rufus, who hunkered on the dirt floor with backs to the wall, dug in with their tin spoons.

"The grub's damned good."

"Good, hell! It's the best eatin' could be for a man just off'n a hard trail!"

Pike put in the last word. "Fine eating for anybody—on or off a trail. Congratulations to Flo, the cook. Thanks, Flo. Good job."

"It was you who furnished the bear meat, Jack

Pike. And you picked out a tender, plump critter to shoot."

Jenny settled herself in the empty floorspace between Pike and McConnell, and contentedly began spooning in mouthfuls. Flo sat on Pike's other side, between him and Rufus.

McConnell decided not to take offense that Flo seemed to be ignoring him. He couldn't begin to guess the reason, since they'd hit it off so well when they'd screwed back at Graybull. Of course, he had no way of knowing what had happened to her in the weeks since.

Maybe if he found out, Skins thought, he could pinpoint the reason for her seeming skittishness toward him. He knew he'd be talking privately with Pike later. Maybe his old friend could enlighten him about the young woman.

Meanwhile, Pike was explaining for Skins and Rufus how the white women came to be in Eagle Valley. It all had something to do, Pike said, with the fact that there'd been trouble at the Ludlow's Bay camp. Pike had quarreled with LeSage over Flo, and afterward the only safe place for Flo and Jenny was the trappers' camp in Eagle Valley.

To McConnell the story didn't sound complete, but he understood it was because it had been laundered for Brumley's benefit. Nevertheless, "Makes sense to me, Jack," Skins said between bites of meat. He told the women, "Be glad to have the company of you two. Prob'ly every man feels the same."

Flo said nothing, and Jenny's face reddened a bit. But about that time Rufus asked for seconds on the grub, and the talk turned to the outlook on the season's beaver harvest—an important subject.

At an hour or so before sundown, Pike accompanied Skins and Rufus on their walk to the flat
ground where they'd been assigned space. The men
worked up a sweat for a short time, putting up
crude shelters. Skins delayed after Rufus went off
to relieve his bladder, and asked Pike, "All right,
then. So what's the truth about the gals, you old
storyteller."

Ten minutes later, McConnell knew everything
there was to know about the incident involving Flo
and LeSage. He shook his head as it sank in. "You
mean, every one of those damned bush-lopers took
a turn stuffing the poor gal? Raping the shit out
of her? Jesus!" Skins's sympathy went out to Flo
Lipscomb.

"A hell of a thing, even for a woman in her line
of work," Pike stated flatly.

"Still, I don't see why the cold shoulder toward
me that Flo shows—"

"Look, Skins. Wake up. Those two, Jenny and
Flo, share that cabin where we ate supper. At bed-
time the one room gets divided by a hung blanket.
Jenny and I sleep in one end."

"And Flo takes the other."

"Right," Pike said. "But Skins, you've got to real-
ize that something's come over Flo since her gang
rape and beating. Something having to do with why
she went after Charbeau—fear of being without
money. Her whole Oregon stake got stolen. My
guess is, she'd planned to get to the settlements,
turn respectable. Now she's determined as hell to
earn back everything she lost and more!"

McConnell stopped in the path they strolled, exhaled a vapor cloud lit by starlight. "Christ, Pike, you don't mean—?"

"I *do* mean. Take a look, Skins."

Beyond a leafless clump of aspens, a woman in a coat—a woman of Flo Lipscomb's size—hurried along, head bowed. "Now, where's she going, Pike?" Skins said. "I know you got an idea."

"If she goes where she's gone most nights, she's headed for one or another of the fellas' lodges. To ply her trade among the men, earn gold. Now, I'm the booshway of this camp, but I don't feel I've got the right to stop her. I'm responsible for her being here."

"Responsible, hell. If it weren't for you, she'd be dead."

Jack Pike shrugged. "Maybe it's a good thing you've come, Skins." He slapped his friend's back. "I know *I'm* glad to see you."

"Tomorrow we'll go over some beaver grounds?"

Pike grinned in the darkness. "Can't wait to start setting trap lines? Yeah, Skins, I'll take you around in the morning. Expect to like what you see."

Chapter 15

" 'Lo, Gap-Tooth."

"Why, goddamn! If'n it ain't Skins McConnell! When'd ya ride in, y'old pizzer-packer?"

Skins peered into the old mountain man's eyes. They reflected the blue of the sky canopying Eagle Valley. Gap-Tooth Williams looked hale and hearty, easily fit for another harsh wintering in the mountain beaver grounds.

"Got in yesterday," McConnell answered. "Threw up my own lean-to last evening, slept in it last night. A buffalo robe pinned across some poles, but you know me, always making the work easy. This morning did some riding around with Jack."

It had indeed been a profitable forenoon. Pike had shown Skins a dozen and more beaver lakes, made numerous suggestions Skins had decided to take. Now McConnell stood outside beside Eagle

Creek—which ran through the camp—sorting traps, inspecting chains, greasing the metal with hand-softened bear fat.

"When ya get done with yer gear, stop by my hut," Gap-Tooth invited. "Li'l hide-covered lodge like the Ute Injuns build theirselves. The kind of by-hisself livin' this coon likes." He dropped a shrewd wink. "Got me a jug of squeezings I'll share with ya, Skins. Stop by before she's all drunk up, hear?"

"Thanks, Gap. I'll take you up on your invite. One of these days."

As the old-timer ambled off, McConnell stamped snow from his double-weight moccasins. It had snowed lightly in the night, and the ground was covered by a fresh, white dusting. Then, he blurted an abrupt "Oh-oh." Around the corner of the nearby trapper's hut stepped Flo Lipscomb, walking fast. She clutched her blanket coat across her chest, and tufts of sorrel poked out from under her fur hat. "Howdy, Flo," Skins finished up lamely.

"Skins! Er, howdy to you, too." She held her lips tight, and their eyes weren't meeting. "Well, I got to hurry. Nice running into you." She moved off stiffly along the path between some hutches, was gone as quickly as she'd appeared.

"Goddamn!" Skins swore.

Glancing around, he saw no one was nearby to hear him.

From the window of the cabin across the flat, Jenny looked out. "Poor Skins," the woman said, letting the oilskin flap fall back in place. She glanced over at Pike where he sat. "Flo met him just now in the yard, and breezed past with hardly a word. As for him, he looks a little hangdog."

Pike shifted on his stool, the long-barreled Hawken resting across his lap. He was cleaning the gun, although it didn't particularly need the attention. As he rubbed bear grease over the smooth iron, he said to the woman, "Skins would do best to stick to his business these days. He's got trap lines to set out. Better them than a woman who goes around acting strange." He paused, then added, "This morning I took him to look over the north end of the valley. He's excited about the season ahead."

Jenny looked at the big man, and smiled impishly. "A fella doesn't work *every* hour of every day. You oughtta know that by now, Pike. In fact, most men need what you need: soft arms to wrap 'em at night. Soft titties to get their blood stirred up—"

"Like you're stirring mine now?" Pike grinned. "You mean that Skins needs female companionship? Or do you mean something else?"

Because the interior of the cabin was so snug and warm, Jenny wore a thin cotton shift that came to her waist—and absolutely nothing else. Her high, round breasts thrust out the clinging fabric, and below the hem could be seen her curving hips and tummy. Her pubic triangle was a tawny, curly bush.

Pike calmly laid aside his rifle.

She plumped playfully down into his lap. "Let's not waste this chance, Pike! Flo'll be out for at least an hour. We've got the cabin to ourselves."

"There's a gun I should be cleaning, vials of castoreum bait to check for potency . . ."

"Poo to work, Jack Pike!" She planted a kiss squarely on his mouth.

Under his trouser fly, he felt his penis go wagon-spoke hard.

"Gal, you *do* know how to persuade a fella."

He lurched to his feet, tugging the woman along. But she slipped from his arms, and trotted to the window. "What we're doing in here, nobody needs know." She allowed the pinned-back blanket to fall into place, blocking the window and foiling peepers. Then, she shed her one and only garment. She paraded totally nude before the manliest man she'd known, well aware of the effect she was having.

And that effect was plenty!

Reveling in her gorgeous nakedness, Jenny worked at undoing Pike's buckskins, freeing what his fly restrained. His erection popped free. For his part, Pike teased the rosettes of the woman's breasts, suckling and running his tongue over them. Meanwhile, she caressed his rigid flagpole, encircling and drawing him.

"Good idea, this." He held her in his arms, lowered her to the bedroll. The furs they sank onto were soft.

"Y'know, Pike, I think I've got something that might interest you—"

He looked at her glisteningly wet crotch, was able to hold back no longer.

Parting her thighs wide with a knee, he fell on her, driving into her pulsing softness.

"Ah," he grunted.

"Ah-ahh!" she sighed.

He worked at her with slow strokes, and felt fine doing so.

Out in the yard McConnell spotted the covered cabin window. He knew full well what Pike and Jenny were doing in there. "Phew!" He spat on the frosty ground. How long had it been since he, Skins, had enjoyed a woman? A month, at least. Long enough so that female companionship was constantly on his mind. But not only his mind was troubled—his balls felt about to burst.

He scowled down at the trap he was holding, then tossed it into a burlap sack with some others and stalked off to find his hobbled packhorse.

Chapter 16

The rider urged his underweight roan steadily through the gentle fall of snowflakes, his potato nose reddened by cold, his hands numb inside gloves a bit too light for this first real onset of winter. Although visibility was far from good, through the white blur he could now see stumps and felled logs piled on the bank of a frozen stream. Some sharpened logs had been planted upright, the beginning of a palisade. Between the palisade and the stream, a village of tents and hide-covered huts was laid out in straight rows.

A brigade men's camp, for sure, if Ab Walsh recognized one when he saw it. Almost certainly the place was the site of the new trading post he'd ridden a long trail to find.

Another thing the horseman noted: the brigade's booshway would need to drive his men if this post was to be ready by spring. But Baptiste LeSage just might be the man to pull it off for the Ludlow's Bay folks.

Although he'd never met the scar-faced Canadian, Walsh knew him by reputation. LeSage was said to rule by fear, a method approved by Walsh, who was of a kindred nature. Walsh expected to hit it off with LeSage when they came face to face. He had information LeSage would be grateful for, plus additional services to offer.

LeSage would be a fool to turn him down.

Six days earlier, up Flaming Canyon way, Walsh had run into a mountain man he knew slightly, Elijah Rowe. From Rowe he'd heard the news that Tim Flanagan was facing ruin. According to Rowe, Ludlow's Bay was moving in on the trader's business, and Baptiste LeSage was supervising construction of that company's trading post. And if Flanagan lost out, claimed Rowe, so would the free trappers.

Rowe also told Walsh of Jack Pike's plan of banding trappers together for a season in Eagle Valley. Come spring, the plan was, together the men would move their furs out, defeat LeSage's brigade force, reward Flanagan with their fur harvest.

Ab Walsh doubted that LeSage knew yet of Pike's plan. Being the first to give him the information, Walsh stood to gain plenty—he hoped.

The wind, picking up, had driven flecks of snow into the long winter hair of Walsh's mount. Walsh, tall in the saddle, was also caked with white. It would be good to get warm again in LeSage's quarters. Surely the booshway would offer a chilled-to-the-bone traveler a drink . . .

Abruptly, a sentry stepped into the horse's path. "Ho!" he shouted, and Walsh reined up. "Who be you?" the kid called out. "State your business! And remember, th' company don't feed no grub-line beggars!"

"I've come to see LeSage. Take me to him."

"You gotta be—"

"You heard me! *Take me to LeSage!*" Walsh jerked out from under his coat a primed Kentucky pistol. Now the weapon came level, aimed directly at the kid's chest. The kid let fall his own firearm. Tears of frustration sprang to his eyes.

Ab Walsh rasped, "You takin' me to yer booshway, or no? If'n the answer's no—"

"Don't shoot me! Please don't shoot!"

"Then you hike on ahead of me into camp. This gun, it'll stay pointed at yer tailbone. When we get to where LeSage hangs his hat, just tell the fella he's got company! Savvy?"

"I savvy!"

"Then let's go, kid. I do need to meet your boss."

In the middle of the camp stood the only structure that had been thrown up to date. The main trading-post building, when finished, would have several rooms, with shuttered windows and a shingle roof. But all that was in the future. Now Baptiste LeSage stood out front, an irritated gleam in his one eye as he watched the stranger ride up.

"*Sacrebleu*, can I get no peace?" the booshway growled. "I must ask you, *monsieur*, to vacate Ludlow's Bay land. And if you don't go willingly—"

Walsh butted in boldly. "You'd best talk to me, LeSage. I know a thing or two that you don't know.

There's work to be done only I can do for you. You kick me out, see, you hurt yourself."

The scar-face scowled. "You two-bit son of a *cochon!*" He raised a hand, as if to signal. Several bystanders' heads turned.

"Jack Pike," Ab Walsh pronounced distinctly.

"What did you say?"

"Jack Pike. I got things to tell about Jack Pike. You interested?"

LeSage's expression subtly changed, a slight purpling around his empty eye socket, somewhat of a curl to the cruel lips. "Pike? What you know of Pike, stranger?"

"Ain't you goin' to ask me inside?" Walsh snapped. "Offer me some firewater? I hear you Frenchies got a grape brew as strong as corn likker. Called candy . . . er, or brandy?"

"Eh bien! Follow me inside!" He turned to the sentry, "Wait here! See we're not interrupted!" The Canadian ducked inside, Walsh following. As soon as the door swung closed, LeSage barked, "All right. Out with what you have to tell me."

Walsh opened his coat, stripped off his well-worn raccoonskin cap. LeSage saw a man whose chest and shoulders were bulky and bulging. But above them rode a face so small it had the quality of a boy, or a dwarf. Even with a thatch of ink black hair, his head was small in proportion to his body. But the deep-pitched voice had the ring of thunder. "Pike's a man you oughtta hate," boomed Walsh. "If'n you don't already. You ain't heard yet what he's up to, I'll bet. Seems there's this place where beaver are still plenty, Eagle Valley, it's called—"

*　*　*

Half an hour later, LeSage knew everything Walsh did. Now, his face twisted in a pleased grimace, he thumped his new friend on the back, and again offered the silver-chased brandy flask. "Good information, Walsh," he said. "Have another drink. We'll toast to the downfall of Pike, and to the success of Ludlow's Bay Company! I agree completely to your plan, and will pay the full reward you ask!"

Walsh took a swallow of the liquor. It burned its way down his innards, hit bottom and smoldered. It was good booze, and his head buzzed pleasantly. "Looks like we got us a partnership, Baptiste."

The man clinked mugs.

"The less delay now, the better," LeSage said. "The big snows will be closing the high mountain passes. How soon can you leave for this Eagle Valley?"

"How's first thing in the morning sound, booshway?"

"That's good. And if Pike has with him the two white women? You'll betray them with the rest?"

"A deal's a deal, Mon-sewer Ludlow's Bay booshway." Walsh's grin was wickedly sly. "And like you just said, we got us one."

Chapter 17

The Indian subchief Black Feather, experienced in years and a courageous man, was restless—more restless than ever in his life. He stood before the lodge his wife and grown daughter had erected, looked across the swale that separated the Snake encampment from that of the whites. Not that the trappers he worked for weren't trustworthy. He'd known Jack Pike for years, knew that the word of He-Whose-Head-Touches-the-Sky could be counted on.

Pike had hired Black Feather and his fellow-tribespeople to guide packhorses with supplies up to the valley. After that, they'd been given the option of staying the winter, in order that there'd be no shortage of hands when it came time to pack out. Black Feather was accompanied by his immediate family: his wife and two offspring. The amount he was being paid was good, both in blankets and other trade goods. The food was likely to be good, too. In the sheltered valley, game abounded.

No, the trouble wasn't with Pike or his deal, but something else.

Last night, when ghostly winds whipped about his lodge and the gentle snowflakes fell, Black Feather had had a dream.

This much he remembered: the dream had been vivid and complicated. Now Black Feather couldn't get it off his mind. It had featured an owl, and he'd awakened in a sweat.

Ever since that morning his edginess had grown, not only for himself, but his wife, their son Brown Turtle—aged twelve summers—their daughter Summer Rain—a maiden of marriageable age. The question was, did trouble really lie ahead, as the dream portended? Should he try to get his family out of danger?

Now the warrior stood in the white drift before his lodge, and scanned the circle of tall peaks that framed the valley. The bright sun gave little warmth at this season. What to do about the alarming nightmare? He'd given his vow to He-Whose-Head-Touches-the-Sky, promising he'd stay all winter. If he let down Pike, word would spread. Throughout the villages, disgrace would fall upon Black Feather.

He heard his squaw Dancing Quail call to him from inside the lodge, and not wanting to talk to her, he moved off. It seemed a good time to go tend his horses.

He trudged off muttering about owls, and the fact that dreaming of them was *very* bad medicine.

As Black Feather sidled away, Summer Rain emerged from the lodge with her brother. Brown Turtle carried his child-sized bow and handful of arrows. "I don't think your father wants you to go off hunting," she told the pest. Like all boys, this one had goals. At present he wanted to kill a deer on his own, because when he did so, he'd be able to take the credit, and appear more a man throughout the Snake encampment.

Both the youngsters were bundled in fur robes: the boy in wolverines' skins and the girl in a cow buffalo's soft hide.

"Brown Turtle, go back inside," the young woman commanded.

"Where are *you* going?" Brown Turtle asked in his adolescent voice that cracked.

"To fetch water from the spring. There's supper to cook."

"I don't want to eat any dried-out old meat."

"There *is* no fresh meat today. You'll eat what's on hand and like it."

As the young woman tramped through the snow, she couldn't help smiling. Bending over the spring, she filled her mother's kettle, acquired years ago from a white trader who'd traveled among the Indian villages. Before she started back to the lodge, she let the surface of the water smooth until it was capable of reflecting a person's features.

The young woman paused to gaze at her reflection.

Summer Rain's face was a pleasing oval, her complexion bronzed and smooth as silk. The young woman's braids, tied with doeskin whangs, glistened like ravens' wings. Several courting braves, speaking their hearts, had called her beautiful. Accepting the compliments, she'd believed the hot-blooded suitors. But as yet she had accepted none of the marriage proposals.

Back at the lodge, her mother asked, "Where's Brown Turtle?"

"Isn't he here? Well, then he's gone hunting, new snow or no new snow! And with his little boy's bow. I'd best take the pinto and track the pest. Don't worry, I'll bring him back."

Dancing Quail watched her daughter mount the mare, tightening her horsehair rein when the horse slipped on an icy patch. Like most people who knew Summer Rain, her mother thought her a sweet maiden. But she was an independent one as well—so much so she hadn't taken a husband yet.

And that wasn't good.

The squaw returned to her cooking for her own man, who always seemed to come home hungry. Among the Snake people, a woman's work was never done.

Chapter 18

The pond was twenty yards wide and a hundred yards long, with four stick-and-mud beaver lodges mounding above the open water near the center. This part of the valley flattened out into a marshy area, where the runoff of springs converged to form the headwaters of a main creek. A limestone lip ran along the bottom of a bulge in the mountain that overlooked the flat, now sprinkled with white.

Jack Pike and Skins McConnell swung from their horses, hauling trap sacks from behind their saddles and, carrying their rifles, plodded through ankle-deep snow down to the bank.

The trained mounts stood calmly, rumps to the wind, their reins grounded.

"So we don't risk dropping our powder in the water," Pike muttered, leaning the Hawken against a beaver-gnawed stump, sweeping the snow with his sleeve from a flat rock. Only then did he take the powder horn off his shoulder and set it atop the almost-dry flat.

"There are plenty of beaver tunnels along here. Let's get to work." Each man selected a trap and a green willow stake from his bag, and walked to the bank. Pike trudged right and Skins hiked left, and soon each found evidence of beaver trails. Pike used a heavy rock to break through the thin ice formed along the pond's edge.

To each trap was attached a three-foot length of wire. Pike straightened out his wire, wrapped one end around a heavy rock he'd used to break the ice. Depressing the heavy spring with his foot, he set the trap, then lowered it beneath the surface. Kneeling at the water's edge, he laid out the chain. He put the stake through the ring at the end of the chain, shoved it into the ground until firmly planted.

"Ready to move on yet, Jack?"

"Almost ready." Pike leaned down, lowered and laid the rock on the submerged ledge next to the trap. "There." When the trap snapped and caught a beaver, the animal would give a jerk and dislodge the rock. The rock would sink, dragging the beaver straight to the bottom. The animal would drown before being able to twist off its foot.

"Now for the last step," Pike mumbled.

With his big hands, he snapped off a sapling branch. From his pocket he took a small vial, fashioned from the tip of an antelope horn. This he uncapped, freeing the pungent odor of castoreum. Pike applied to one end of the branch an amount of the fluid from a beaver's castoreum gland. Then he drove the branch down alongside the trap, its scented end sticking up above the water.

"Can't you move faster?" McConnell called, good-naturedly.

"What's your rush?"

"I'm cold."

"But there isn't even much snow on the ground. At least, not yet."

"Believe me, Jack, I'm glad of that. Oh, I like the income to be got from trapping, but not the discomfort, Why hell, I'd as soon be—"

"Shacked up in a heated cabin? With a woman? Screwing merrily away?"

McConnell laughed. "All right, so you can read minds. What else is new, Jack? Say, are we setting out lines along this lakeside or aren't we?"

Just then the noise of a scream pierced the silence of the valley. Almost immediately, there followed a shrill animal snarling, as unearthly a sound as either man had ever heard.

"What the hell's that?" Skins blurted.

"It came from the woods on that hillside! Let's go!"

Two minutes later the men reined in under trees, their heads and shoulders brushing snow from low overhanging branches. More snow was lofted in clouds by skidding horses' hooves. Pike and McConnell flung themselves from their saddles, guns ready, and dashed into the trees. There was a young Snake woman half-buried in a white drift, looking far from chipper. Her deerskin skirt and leggings were smeared with blood, and the surrounding snow was spattered with crimson.

Summer Rain's eyes were wide with terror. In front of her she clutched a sharp, wide-bladed skinning knife.

Pike dropped to his knees beside her. "What happened?"

From her association over the years with white traders, she knew quite a bit of English. "A big cat— the kind you whites call mountain lion! It jumped out and scared me! Who wouldn't have been scared? The animal came out of the rocks, took a great swipe at me with its claws!"

The woman's face was tight with pain, Pike saw. Noting that she leaked blood from her right leg, he reached into his pocket for a length of whang leather with which to fashion a tourniquet . . .

"The gal's telling the truth!" McConnell called from yards off, the grove's edge. "I found the critter's tracks, plus pony tracks and deer tracks! The deer and the painter cat have skedaddled, and I'm following the pony tracks now!"

Pike questioned the woman further. "You were riding and came on the deer, is that what happened?"

"I was looking for a boy, my brother," Summer Rain said. "But then the doe ran across the pony's path. Then the cat suddenly sprang from those big rocks. It caught me with a sweep of its claws, then fastened on the pony that bolted off."

"I see," Pike grunted. "Likely the painter was hunting the critter, and that's how you happened to tangle with it." He was working at tearing away her hip-high leggings, now slippery with melted snow and blood. When the deerskin came away, her calf was exposed—only a bit mangled, with three inch-long tears in the dusky skin. It was clear they'd been inflicted by a predator's sharp claws.

"I got to say you're lucky, er—?"

"I am called Summer Rain."

"Pleased to meet you, Summer Rain. I'm Jack Pike, and my friend over there, that's Skins McConnell. I was going to call you lucky, but I changed my mind. Actually, you're *very* lucky. I don't see you coming out of this crippled—"

"Pike," shouted Skins. "The moccasin tracks the gal was following—the brother's—lead out of the woods, so the kid's likely long-gone and safe. As for her pony, I'm looking down at it. And it's one messy piece of horse flesh!"

Pike got up and walked over to McConnell. His friend was standing at the lip of a gully, peering down at yet another snowdrift. This one ugly with the presence of a half-buried dead mare. What stuck above the snow—the head, neck and forequarters—had been raked by ferocious teeth and claws. The gouges were deep and terrible.

But that wasn't the worst. Above walleyes frosted in death, the entire top of the horse's head had been ripped off. In one tremendous bite. The big cat's massive jaws had clamped, the horse's blood and brains had sprayed the area. The surrounding snow was dyed as red as a slaughterhouse floor.

Pike shrugged. "A big painter, for damn sure, to be able to chomp like that." He and McConnell trudged back to where Summer Rain lay, nursing her pain.

"We'll help her back among her people," Pike was saying, but McConnell interrupted.

"I just thought of something."

"Yeah, Skins?"

"That painter could be the biggest cat in all these mountains. And from what the gal said, it wasn't scared of humans—not even a little! Pike, this valley's that cat's home, its hunting territory!"

Pike wagged his big head from side to side.

"This *could* turn into a damned tough winter, all right."

Chapter 19

In Black Feather's elkhide-covered winter lodge, Summer Rain sat alone and stared at the smoke-stained walls at midday. Atop a bed of soft furs, her lap covered by a fluffy buffalo robe, she was comfortable, but rather bored. She missed Dancing Quail and Brown Turtle, whom she was used to having around. Her father had shot an elk that morning, then had come and taken his wife and son back with him into the hills. Together out there, they'd dress the meat and pack it back to camp.

Summer Rain's leg hurt less, this day after she'd had the run-in with the cougar. The poultice of herbs her mother had applied was doing its job, and the claw wounds seemed to be healing nicely.

Now she dropped on her lap her awl and the moccasin to which she'd been applying some porcupine-quill decoration. By looking upward through the smoke hole of the lodge, she could see the

118

bright blue sky, which set her to thinking about the two white men she'd met the afternoon before. She wondered if Pike and McConnell were out reaping a good catch at trapping.

As the fire in the pit burned further down, she found herself tugging her robe higher under her pretty chin. And the warmth and the musky animal smell made her drowsy.

She was about to nod off, when she heard the scratching outside the door flap. Who was there? She picked up the skinning knife from the dirt floor.

"Summer Rain? You at home?" The voice was masculine, deep-pitched. "It's me, Skins McConnell. We met yesterday. Just thought I'd stop by, see how you are. Mind if I come in?"

Her heart leaped. Since her family wasn't due back much before sundown, she'd looked forward to a dull afternoon at best. Now she'd have a good-looking man to be entertained by.

"Yes, Skins," she called out. "I mean, yes, I'm here, and yes, you can come in!"

She quickly sat up and arranged her necklace of glass trader's beads—of which she was proud—and the long black braids she let fall down her dress front. McConnell entered, crossed the swept floor, crouched beside her. By this time she'd coyly cast her eyes down.

"Feeling better?"

"Yes."

"But you're not healed enough yet to be up and at your usual work?"

"No." She studied him with her dark, alert eyes. Skins was a lean but solidly built man under his clean, neat buckskins. Of the white men she'd seen,

119

only Jack Pike—He-Whose-Head-Touches-the-Sky—was taller, heavier-muscled and looked more graceful when he moved. But she'd seen Pike in the company of his woman of blond hair and blue eyes, and had sensed their closeness. And Skins McConnell, as far as Summer Rain knew, had chosen no woman in the valley to share his living quarters. In other words, he wasn't attached.

So that was why he acted as he did toward Summer Rain. He was doing little things for her now—her, an Indian girl laid up with injuries from an encounter with a catamount. "Getting cold in the lodge, isn't it?" Skins asked. "Shall I stir up the fire?" Before she could answer he moved to the pit, stirred some of the coals with a stick, laid some twigs over the embers and fanned them with his hand. Small yellow flames began playing from the red coals. The yellow spread and blazed up. Skins added more wood, and with warmth beginning to radiate, made his way back to the side of the woman.

She'd thrown back her robe, and held out her arms to him. Her eyes sparkled with desire, her full lips parted. "Come, Skins," she said in a husky voice. "My family is gone now, but they'll return. We must make the most of our time."

"Your leg don't bother you too much to—?"

"Don't talk so much, Skins! Just come to Summer Rain!"

Her hands found the ties of his buckskin shirt, and when his garment was peeled back, she began divesting herself of her own clothes. As she shucked down her dress, Skins noted the deep cleft between her breasts, the gentle tummy bulge, the scant dark pubic patch.

· As McConnell undid the buttons of his fly, the woman kissed his cheek and purred, "Let me." Her fingers spidered over his shoulders and chest, and he decided to touch her, too. His hands roamed her breasts, and twin dark nipples bloomed. She interrupted his caress long enough to slip off his britches. Then she snatched at his throbbing manhood as it sprang up. Swarming into his arms, she pressed her lips to his lips.

Aching need throbbed in McConnell's groin. He felt his restraint going . . . going . . . gone!

He lowered his head and nuzzled her belly. He lapped her as a heifer laps a salt lick, and her body trembled with arousal. "Oh, Skins," she mewed. "You are a real man! Fit to be my first! Teach me the secrets of what men do to women."

"This is your first time? I don't want to hurt you, Summer Rain."

"The greatest hurt is not having you!"

Summer Rain spread her legs, eager to receive his maleness. McConnell positioned himself, laid his throbbing cock against her oozing cleft. Slowly, delightfully, he worked the sensitive tip against her slit. He shuddered, but kept himself from exploding.

The woman moaned happily.

McConnell lowered himself onto her. He pushed into her hot, wet portal.

She gasped with delight and pawed at him. Encountering the obstacle that was her maidenhead, he shoved and probed, then desisted.

"Summer Rain, I—"

"It's all right, Skins. I want you very badly. Take me!"

He probed her again with the tip of his impatient

phallus. With each short stroke he felt the obstacle membrane give, as if yielding its hold on her virginity. Then plaintively she wailed, "Oh, Skins! Don't make me wait more!"

With a powerful heave, McConnell impaled her. Her hymen gave way, ripped by his force. She cried out, then embraced him, as he burrowed to her depths, bottoming. All the while, her hips were pumping frantically.

What they shared was incredible. Summer Rain threw her head back and wailed. Then her body spasmed with orgasm. Waves of sensation broke in tides. She rocked with McConnell, thrashed as the climaxes washed her.

Skins's own frenzied fulfillment came, jolting him. Creamy seed jetted into her.

She lay relaxed under him, and sighed. "Ah, Skins, it was so—"

"Good?"

"Better than good. The earth moved! Oh, Skins!"

He was about to withdraw, but she grabbed his shoulders. Her ankles locked around his lean waist.

"Aw, honey! I just now gave my all. A man, he can't just—"

"You can't do it again right away, Skins? Are you sure?"

Her fluttering hands went at him eagerly, and again his cock grew enormous. "Well-l-l, I reckon I can, at that."

"Oh, Skins! Oh, Skins! Oh, yes, *yes-s-s-s!*"

They rode to glory a second time.

And it wasn't even the last time that day.

Chapter 20

The steep upslope trail wasn't only narrow, it was uneven, full of rocks and depressions under the snow. In places it was covered with deep drifts. Ab Walsh pushed his roan with little mercy, feeling the harsh wind in his face. The packhorse was drawn along, balky on its lead. When Walsh lifted his gaze to the sky, he saw fat, low clouds, heavy and iron gray.

The really big snows in the mountain wouldn't be holding off much longer, he felt. And the scruffy Arkansan did a lot of relying on his hunches.

This trail led to higher elevations, toward Eagle Pass, which led to Eagle Valley. Walsh would get there before the big snow, if he was lucky.

And then he'd meet Jack Pike.

And with Pike it would be a question of luck all over again.

Maybe Pike wouldn't suspect his motives.

Wouldn't guess he was now working for LeSage. In other words, Pike might be a pushover.

This was Walsh's hope.

However, Jack Pike was known the length and breadth of the Shining Mountains. Called by the Indians He-Whose-Head-Touches-the-Sky, Pike was known as a person who was hard to fool. And in a fight he was as formidable as they came—right up there with Jim Bridger and Tom Fitzpatrick and Milt Sublette, all mountain men who'd survived hundreds of deadly scrapes.

But although Walsh had crossed paths with Pike before, he'd never met him head-on as an antagonist. Who could say how things would turn out in the days ahead?

The important thing about the Arkansan was, he believed in his own invincibility. In this way he was different from LeSage, who combined deviousness and cunning, with caution.

But like LeSage, Ab Walsh would stop at nothing. Thanks to his deal with LeSage, he was on the Ludlow's Bay Company payroll, earning a fat sum. Plus, if he came out on top against Pike, there'd be bonuses. Walsh couldn't afford to lose.

Now, at the juncture of two rugged trails, his horse stumbled in deep snow, so he dismounted, leading the balky animal. He could see, across the next saddleback, the pass that was his destination. He forged ahead. He came to a place where the wind had scoured the snow beneath a low ridge line. But the rocks and soil wore a coat of ice.

The ice had recently been broken by a horse's hooves.

Noting this, Ab Walsh caught a whiff of campfire

smoke. He was hungry, he was cold, and the day was fading into early winter dusk. He gigged the roan toward a line of trees, and the smell of smoke grew stronger. He could see a blaze of a small fire.

He reined in his horse, and called out, "Howdy!"

"Howdy, yerself. Ride on in."

"Obliged." Walsh stepped from leather and advanced, his hand poised inches from his belt where his Kentucky pistol rode. Then he spotted the camper and relaxed. "Iz? Israel Potter?"

"I'll be damned! If'n it ain't Ab Walsh! Put yer horse up, and set yer ass on down! I about got supper cooked!"

Potter was an old mountain man, well known throughout the Bitterroots as a generous, friendly soul. Even friendly with Walsh. Ab had nothing whatsoever against him.

When Walsh had unsaddled and hobbled his two horses, he hunkered at the fire, warming himself. "Smells like bacon and biscuits."

"Ya ain't wrong," the old-timer acknowledged. "Got coffee too. In m' pack, if'n ya care to fetch th' bag of beans."

Ab Walsh enjoyed coffee, so he got up, plodded to the old man's saddle pack, began pawing through bags of potatoes and flour and rice. When he found the coffee beans, he snatched up the bag and started to turn—when his glance fell on an interesting non-edible object. His shrewd eyes examined his find.

It was a powder horn. But *what* a powder horn! From tip to end and around its bend it was decorated with carving: elaborate waves, swirls, curlicues. There was even a picture of a hunter and a buffalo. The depicted man was shooting at the depicted beast. A drawn puff of smoke rolled from the inch-long represented gun barrel.

From over Ab's shoulder Potter's voice reached him. "Why ya slow, lad? Ya lookin' at m' horn? Helluva horn! Pictures carved in it by my Clem. He's th' middle of m' three sons."

"Don't reckon you'd care to part with the piece?"

"Nope. Them three sons o' mine, they're all stout lads. I aim to see 'em in a few days, up to Eagle Valley. But for now, Ab, what say we eat?"

Later, over a waning fire, Walsh said, "Good grub." As Iz Potter peered at Ab's small pixy face, Ab gave a loud belch. "M' belly, it's tight as a Sioux shaman's drum. Had me a hard day on the trail, Iz, so I reckon I'll turn in." He spread his soogans, and soon was faking snores.

A bit later, Israel bedded down, too.

Before the hour was out, the old man awoke, to look up at Walsh looming over him. The Arkansan had out his heavy horse pistol, the barrel gleaming in the dying fire's glow. It looked as if Iz was going to die too. "What ya up to, Ab? Not murder? Hell, I shared m' coffee and grub! Never done nothin' to ya!"

"You got a powder horn I admire, old man! So good-bye to you!" The pistol's shot shattered the night, Israel Potter was flung back, his body lurching at the impact from the ball. He lay on the ground, screaming from a gut wound, as Ab snatched up the horn, ran his fingers over the smooth lines.

"Ungrateful bastard," the old man groaned. "I shared my grub, and ya—" His feeble voice trailed

126

off. He lay in the snow, hugging his bleeding abdomen. His face was ghost white above his beard.

"I don't reckon I'll waste more powder and shot on you, old man!" Grabbing Israel Potter's ankles, Walsh dragged him along the frozen ground. Beyond the boulders lay a gulch, a good burying spot.

"Jesus! What now?"

"You're dyin' too slow."

Potter caterwauled and clawed at the ground, trying to get away from Ab. Walsh broke into a sweat as he manhandled the bleeding man past the remains of the fire. The old-timer thrashed as he was dragged, one of his arms flopping through the fire, igniting his sleeve. Now Iz howled with panic as well as pain, pounding his arm against the ground to beat out flames. Walsh walked backwards to the edge of the gulch, pulling the old-timer.

Potter screamed and begged as Ab Walsh dipped low to get a better grip. Walsh's sour breath was in the victim's nostrils, mingling with the stink of his own spilled blood and entrails. When he persisted in resisting, Walsh stomped and kicked the old man. When he squawked in agony, Walsh kicked and stamped until the old man's midsection was hammered spongy.

Walsh shoved Iz from the lip, but the old man clung with gnarled hands.

Walsh picked up a jagged stone and beat at Potter's hands. The sharp rock sliced off two fingers, and blood geysered. Soon gashes covered the hand as Walsh kept up. Then the hand released its grip, and the old man went limp.

Iz Potter was dead.

The clouds parted for a moment, and Walsh surveyed what he'd gained. There was the fancy powder horn, of course, but also two extra horses, a hefty supplies pack. The pack undoubtedly held beaver traps.

Walsh had a thirst for coffee, but was too lazy to build up the fire. So he simply turned in, pulling around him Iz Potter's wolfskin.

Walsh slept soundly, and without dreams.

Chapter 21

Jack Pike and Skins McConnell, over years of working together, had become a good team. Now today, near Eagle Valley's main entrance pass, the two mountain men worked one of their trap lines with little enough fuss. The cheeks of both men were ruddy from cold, and a wind blew swirling snow into their beards whenever they faced north.

Skins skirted the iced edge of the pond as he walked toward Pike, in his hands the limp body of a wet, dead beaver. Pike eyed the fur with pleasure and stroked it. "I'd call this a prime pelt, Skins. You get the trap all reset back there?"

"That I have, Jack. Ready to move on. Looks like you haven't done so bad either."

Pike showed his own catch, which consisted of three dripping, paddle-tailed carcasses. "Let's see, *you've* taken three, and *I've* got three. At fifteen dollars a pelt . . . that comes out to exactly sixty dollars. More than a month's wages for a man back in the East. So we're doing all right."

"*If* the trading price for fur holds up," Skins reminded.

"Oh it will, it will," Pike said. "We'll help out Tim Flanagan and his Graybull post, and Tim'll help us. Best thing we could've done, coming this year up to Eagle Valley."

"Fifty-three mountain men in the valley, and not a smidgen of trouble out of 'em, so far."

"Of course, the hard part of winter hasn't set in yet. I'm keeping my fingers crossed, pard. Plenty of fellas haven't got *our* way of relaxing in the evening. They play cards, that's all."

McConnell grinned. "While we've got ourselves Jenny and Summer Rain—"

Pike caught sight of a movement back in a juniper grove. "Hate to interrupt, Skins, but look!" Pike pointed to a rider whose horse was breaking a drift to reach them. The man was shaggy-bearded and trail-worn, with pack animals at lead. The stranger raised a gloved hand in greeting.

"Up till today fifty-three white trappers. Mark down another in the tally, Skins," Pike said. The newcomer came within a few yards, reined in and sat his mount.

"Damn, if he doesn't look familiar. I'm thinking maybe I've seen the feller before—"

"I recognize him, Skins. His name's Walsh. Abner Walsh."

"Fellas," the newcomer sang out. "I'm a trapper, name of Ab Walsh." Now the man moved to dismount, swinging his topheavy frame down clumsily. "I've rode a hell of a ways to get to Eagle Valley,

130

join up with the crew. Heard about LeSage and Ludlow's Bay tryin' to twist Tim Flanagan's short hairs. Reckon you boys got the best way to screw LeSage, the polecat."

Pike shook the hand Walsh offered, studied his odd, pixyish face. "Always room for one more," Pike said. "Welcome to Eagle Valley. I'm Jack Pike, and my pard here is Skins McConnell."

"Yeah, our paths have crossed before, Pike. I remember you."

"I guess you could call me the booshway in these parts. We've got us some rules the boys have voted on, but not many. About fistfighting, getting drunk and making trouble—that sort of thing. Any fella wanting to, and with half a wit, can get along."

Walsh bristled. "Hell, I'm more than a half-wit! I'm—" Then he chose to laugh off Pike's words. The scowl vanished from his countenance, replaced by a a smile. "Hell, I don't want trouble. Just a chance this season of a beaver haul."

Pike nodded. "We'll ride over with you to the main camp. Show you where you can pitch your hide shelter, dig you a cache where you can stow your gear." While he talked, Pike tied the beavers to his bay's back. "And you, me and Skins can go over those regulations I mentioned. They're not laws, really, but if you understand 'em it could help in case a fracas crops up among the men—or women."

A look of surprise washed Walsh. "Huh? There's females winterin' here in the valley?"

Pike wound up his speech. "I don't guess you'll be any trouble, Walsh. Put it this way: you won't last long if you try anything bad-assed."

Then Pike turned on his heel and marched to his horse, swung into the saddle. He rode off, letting the other men follow, in the direction of camp.

"Ab Walsh? He's in the valley? My God!"

Jenny Henderson gnawed her lip, drummed her fingers on the table Pike had hammered together for the cabin. As was more and more usual these days, Flo wasn't at home to eat with them.

"You know about Ab and me," Jenny went on. "Hell, when I last saw him he wanted to kill me. So, what do I do now?"

Pike picked up a chunk of beaver tail that had been expertly seasoned, basted with the oil of a wild goose. The big man finished the portion in two bites, then sat back and licked his fingers. "Can't say what you ought to do, Jenny."

The food was delicious. Jenny had even topped her last meal. The food and the hot times in their bedrolls—those were the reasons Pike had been putting off teaching her the trapper's art. Although she'd been complaining that he wasn't letting her learn the trapper's craft, begging to be allowed to come along on checks of his line.

One of these days, he supposed he'd run out of excuses, and be forced to take her. But in the meantime . . .

"Pike, should I hide from Ab?"

Pike remembered what Jenny had told him about her former "protector." The couple had met at Fort Graybull, and when he'd asked her to leave with him for the high country, she'd agreed. Not long

132

after, she'd chosen to make her own way back. Which had put her in the position of needing a horse—there was no other way she could have made it back to civilization. So she'd tried to steal Pike's dun stud.

She hadn't stayed with Walsh long—almost the day they'd left Graybull, the abuse started. Ab was brutal in their couplings, and thought nothing of degrading the woman. He'd begun beating her.

As Pike put it together, Walsh wasn't a man likely to change.

Tonight at the supper table, Jenny looked pretty scared. "I'm worried! The man's a bastard, and I had the bruises to prove it. Going into the woods with a mountain man—at first it seemed so romantic. But how long did it last?"

Pike shrugged.

Jenny peered at him. "Lordy, was Ab mad when I told him I was walking out. Did I tell you he swore he'd kill me?"

"Less than a minute ago." Pike sipped some coffee. "Jenny, you asked if you should hide. I don't guess that'd be possible. The first reason is, most of the trappers around here know you're living with me. Walsh will hear about that from them."

"There's a second reason?"

"This: the fella's standing outside right now. Any minute he'll rap and want to come in."

"Christ, Pike!"

"And I'll let him in. The best thing to do is face him down. If he takes offense that you're here—"

Turning, Jenny could see what Pike had seen. Between a loosened hide flap and cabin frame.

Walsh—big-framed, unmistakable—was indeed standing there. And sure enough, the knock sounded.

"Come on in, Walsh. You're expected."

The visitor ducked inside. "Pike, I'd like to borrow some tools if I might—" Catching sight of Jenny, Walsh froze. Her former male friend looked at her, and she looked back.

Pike gave her credit for acting bold as brass. "How do, Ab?"

The man actually seemed surprised. "Jenny, you here? Damn! I didn't know." Turning to Pike, he remarked, "I see how 'tis—She's your woman now."

Pike had positioned himself against the wall. If an assault came, he'd have room to swing his fists. But the visitor remained calm and kept a straight look on that peculiar little face. No sneer was sneered, no blow was thrown. "Well, gal, you landed on your feet. That's the way it goes, I reckon. No hard feelings."

He addressed Pike, "What I came for is, I've lost my screwdriver. The lock on the rifle, it needs some adjusting."

"I'll lend you my 'driver. Here." Pike slapped the tool into Walsh's palm.

"Obliged. Evenin' now, folks. Be seein' you."

Ab Walsh threw the door hide back, and breezed out into the sunset hour.

"He's gone?"

"He's gone!"

"What a relief! You're wonderful, Jack Pike! He was scared of you, I felt it! You saved my ass!"

"And now that I've saved it, what?"

134

"Celebrate? Sure! Right here on the buffalo robe! Do me!"

As Pike and Jenny flopped atop the bedroll they shared, Ab tromped off through the snow. His poker face had served him well. He hadn't let on. He'd been flabbergasted, but he hadn't let on.

To see her again—and here! Under his breath he growled, "Bitch! Oh, I'll be gettin' even, bitch! You'll get yours!"

And as Ab Walsh grumbled, his brain went to work.

Chapter 22

Pike awoke with a start, lurching upright in the burrow of robes in which he and Jenny slept. It was chilly in the place, and the darkness was cut only by glowing fireplace coals. The curtain that divided the cabin was drawn, and soft snores came from the other side. Flo had come home, and so the hour was late.

But what had disturbed Pike wasn't Flo, but a noise from outside. A faint sound, like a prowling animal. In the reddish glow, Pike looked down at Jenny, asleep beside him. He imagined, more than saw, her curled form. But he could feel her naked thigh against him, under the robes.

Whatever it was outside made another noise. Slight, but worthy of investigating. "Damn," Jack Pike grumbled. He slipped out of the robes, sought his trousers in the almost-dark. He tugged on his buckskin trousers, moccasins and blanket coat.

Stealthily, he moved to the door, opened the hide flap a crack and peeked out. The light was bad; only starshine reflecting off the snow-packed ground. Pike could hardly make out nearby trees and sheds. The big man slipped out through the door flap . . .

Out of the shadows, a hulking, menacing form rushed him! Thanks to a turned-up capote collar, the attacker's face was hidden. Pike whiffed hot whiskey breath, then glimpsed a club rushing toward his head. His hand went up instinctively. He deflected the blow, knocked the club from his opponent's grip.

The man grunted. "You son of a bitch!"

Pike clenched his fists together, brought them down across his foe's back. His hands crunched bone and flesh smacked flesh. The heavyset adversary doubled up, dropped to his knees.

Pike stepped up warily. The man was far from disabled. Your average jasper would have been eating snow, but this bull-shouldered foe was shaking himself. Pike felt an arm lock his leg. It was as if a vise held him—a bone-crushing vise. A hand crawled up Pike's leg toward the groin.

Pike brought his forearm down hard, and something gave. The hold on his leg slackened. But huge gloved hands sought his throat.

Stars flashing his head, Pike dodged, trying to elude the grip. Strong fingers closed on his neck. The pressure made his eyes go dim. Blackness tried to flood his brain.

He'd have to break the grip, or die. *Have* to!

He powered a knee at his enemy's crotch, but missed his target. Nevertheless, the attacker's grip was slackened, and Pike twisted free, danced back. His breaths came in agonized gasps.

The man charged him again!

The shadowy enemy stalked Pike on quick feet. Pike lashed out, burying a fist in his breadbasket. The blow was shaken off like a feather's flick.

The blotlike hulk seemed to advance out of a fog, a mountain about to cave in on Pike. Pike shot out a hard left, connecting. As Pike backed off, his mind raced.

The man was a dangerous fighter, fast for his size, hard-fisted. Pike needed to put him away. Since he was without weapons, that meant with his bare hands. The thing to do was hit and hurt the man.

But where? His fist drove to the other's gut, as if into quicksand. Blows glanced off the man's head, thanks to scarves and a bulky fox-skin cap. But although the man was strong, he had to have a weakness. A soft spot.

Feeling his way step by step, Pike backed to the cabin's wall. With a grunt, his attacker came on, shambling. His head was down, arms spread as if to enfold Pike, then snap his spine.

The enemy launched himself!

When the big opponent ran at him, Pike dodged, and the man's fists crunched into the log wall. Then Pike kicked out, aiming for a kidney. The toe of his moccasin struck something soft, and the attacker jackknifed in agony. Pike brought a fist up from the ground with all his strength.

He'd put his shoulder into the blow, and felt a jarring in his arm as his fist bashed the man's face. The enemy reeled back, almost fell, but at the last minute regained his balance. He trembled all over, as if the breaths wouldn't come. Then he turned and broke into a staggering run.

Pike started to follow, but his foot skidded on a patch of ice, and he almost fell. The attacker was in the trees by now, bulling through, the brush crashing. From the doorway of the cabin, a voice called, bell-like. "Pike? Pike? Are you all right?"

Two tousled heads thrust out, one blond and one sorrel-colored. Jenny's and Flo's.

"Yeah, I'm all right." Pike kicked an ice chunk, and it flew ten yards.

Then he trudged back over the trampled snow, cursing Ab Walsh.

If his attacker really had been Ab Walsh.

Chapter 23

"So let's see what the prowler left," MConnell said. Pike's sidekick flexed shoulders inside his coat. In his right hand he hefted his rifle.

At this early-morning time of day, the mother-of-pearl light had just begun to kiss the mountain tops. The sun was a feeble thing, having just risen.

"Yeah. We do need clues."

Pike was engaged in priming his Hawken afresh, as was his habit when he might be going up against enemies. His thoughts ran along the same lines as Skins's. No sense starting out less than prepared.

There had been few clues. A few blood smears on the ground outside the cabin. Some spilled gunpowder in the snow outside Pike's pelt-drying shed adjacent to the cabin. Nearby had lain a fancy powder horn, the cap knocked off, its contents damp and spoiled. Pike's toe had kicked it when he'd first walked out this morning. Although he'd seen most

140

of the horns belonging to the valley trappers, this particular one he didn't recognize. Now he again showed it to Skins, and together they studied the fine workmanship.

A lot of time had been spent with knife and gouge in creating a true work of art. The horn—originally grown on the skull of a giant ox—was covered from end to end with decorative lines, swirls and, of course, the drawing. The represented buffalo hunter might've been real. The carved gun even appeared to be a Hawken.

"Ever see it before, Skins?"

"Naw."

"Well, we'll ask every fella we run into today. But first, right now, the best chance of finding our man is these tracks."

The snow was trampled for yards around. The fight, obviously, had been fierce while it lasted. The unrecognized opponent had been tough. He'd managed to mark Pike. A puffy, blue bruise rode the big man's cheek like an overgrown mushroom.

So, this morning's job was to find the jasper. And persuade him to confess, and tell just why he'd jumped the booshway of Eagle Valley.

If the perpetrator resisted with killing force, Pike and McConnell might be forced to shoot. That was the reason for all the firepower they carried.

"Could the attacker have been Ab Walsh?" Skins asked.

"Yeah, I figure he's a suspect."

"There hasn't been a speck of trouble in this camp till now, not so much as a bad disagreement over cards. That's remarkable, considering all the trappers. But then Walsh rides in, and the very next day you get jumped."

A nod from the bigger man.

"Jack, last evening Walsh dropped by your cabin, saw Jenny there. Surely he put two and two together, guessed she was *your* woman now."

Pike scanned the footprints of a man leading away from the cabin. Then he took off following them. "Jenny may be my gal, Skins, *but only for the time being*. Our arrangement isn't permanent. She and I don't own each other."

"If you say so. Anyhow, if Jenny kissed Ab off less than a month ago—"

"That part's true, Skins. I believe what the gal told me. And the bruises she carried were real, that night she tried to steal my horse."

McConnell spoke as they pursued the trail into an aspen thicket. "Jack, who *else* can it be but Walsh? The jasper came after you in the middle of the night. Or maybe he was after Jenny."

"Or Flo."

"What's Flo got to do with Walsh?"

"Nothing. That's why I'm not charging straight to Ab's quarters. There's got to be proof he's involved. The man last night could've been a customer of Flo's—one of many. Flo's a 'soiled dove' by trade. Flo doesn't do much talking. Just smiles a lot, gloats over the money she makes hauling men's ashes. God bless the whores—what'd we do without 'em?" Pike fingered his split lip. "Hell, for that matter, the prowler could've been after her coin!"

Skins squinted. "A robbery motive? I doubt that, Jack."

They stood on a hilltop, scanning the far side. Below could be seen scattered trappers' shelters, ranging from semipermanent lean-tos to simple bedrolls spread in the shelter of rock ledges. Housing didn't seem to be a trapper's highest priority. Most worked from dawn to dark, scraping the fat and sinews from fresh pelts, stretching them on willow bows. In addition, they trudged their trap lines every day, reaping the harvest of beavers, otters, martens, mink. Those without women to cook for them—virtually everyone but Pike—survived on jerked venison, muskrat meat, beaver tails scorched hastily over a fire. Some didn't even bother to brew coffee.

Responding to Skins's remark, Pike said, "So you doubt it. Shows we'd better get proof on Walsh before we brace him."

Pike's gaze roamed toward the north—toward the grouped lodges of the Snakes, where McConnell had been at the time of the attack. Then Pike's eyes returned to the ground, the tracks. They led straight ahead and down—directly toward a knot of trappers' horses standing hobbled in the swale.

"You made a deal of law and order when you got to be booshway," McConnell reminded Pike. "You were goin' to run the camp by rules."

"The only way, Skins. I hate to shoot first and ask questions later—although sometimes I'm forced to."

McConnell pointed at a hut of branches and banked earth. "There's where Walsh has been sleeping—not far from Black Feather's lodge. I've seen him coming and going."

"Last night did you—?"

"No, Jack, I didn't see him last night. Summer Rain and I were . . . er, busy."

Pike and McConnell strode downhill, liking less and less of what they saw. It looked as if the trail ended with the horses. For many yards around, the wavy, white perfection of the snow cover had been trampled. The trappers' horses were moved from time to time, but the idea was to allow them to forage, primarily in meadows, where they could paw the snow to find old grass.

Now Pike and Skins saw last night's assailant's tracks obliterated.

"Shit!"

Pike searched in one direction, Skins in another. Beyond the horse-graze area they found more moccasin tracks, but they were many in shape and size, and they formed a maze. By this time of morning, numerous trappers were up and about. A few hailed Pike and Skins cheerily.

"What happened to yore face, booshway?" one whooped.

"Sleep with your rifle, and the stock whomped ya?"

"Fall off your horse?"

"Catch your face in a trap?"

"Sure," Pike laughed. "All those things. Say, anybody seen Ab this morning?"

Elijah Rowe spoke up. "No. And, come to think on it, I usually do by this time. Could he've got drunk, be sleepin' late?"

"Me and Skins'll go see. Thanks, Elijah." They moved off, Pike saying to McConnell: "I had to've marked the jasper I fought. Torn his clothes. Something."

Closing in on Walsh's shelter, the men found it hard to see. Outside the bright sun reflected off the snow's glare, but inside it was dim. Pike and Skins sneaked forward with their rifles cocked.

"Walsh? You in there, Walsh?"

A sleepy grumble.

"Get your ass out here, Walsh! You got some explaining to do!"

"Explaining? What the hell you talkin' 'bout?"

The Arkansan appeared, fur cap pushed back, collar flaps loose at the throat. The man's clothing looked undamaged, and the man's small face, although grimy, was free from any cuts or scrapes.

The man didn't look as if he'd been in a fight. With his knuckles he rubbed sleep from his eyes. The knuckles weren't swollen or bruised.

Earlier, Pike had decided: no proof, no accusation. Now Walsh grumbled some more. "Whatcha want, Pike? Christ, I drank too much forty-rod! My head!"

Pike eased down his flintlock's hammer. "Don't have anything to say to you, Walsh."

"Jack's right," McConnell added. "Except to remind you, you got a trap line to walk."

"And so do we. So, so long, Walsh."

Walking back to the cabin McConnell said, "You could've braced him, Jack. I'd have backed you."

"I believe he was behind it, Skins. But I can't be sure."

Back at his bailiwick, Walsh pissed against a tree, hot yellow urine steaming. *Well, he suspects, but he don't know. Gives me another good chance at him, it do. Next time, Jack Pike, me and m'pards, we won't miss you!*

145

Chapter 24

"Ya don't say!"

"Pike come around, all questions?"

"Hell, he killed our poor paw! He's got him a lump of ice for a heart, the son of bitch!"

"And we'll have revenge yet! 'Cause Pike took him the life of old Israel Potter!"

Of the four hunkering around the fire, three were young, ranging from nineteen to twenty-five. The fourth man, Ab Walsh, was in his thirties. Walsh splashed liquor from a squat jug into tin mugs. It wasn't his personal-use spirits; it was cheap trading whiskey he kept on hand for plying Indians—or those whites he regarded as fools.

The crackskull was raw grain alcohol laced with pepper, sweetened with molasses and colored with tobacco juice. Extra bite was given the concoction by the addition of some pickled rattlesnake heads.

Strong stuff.

This afternoon the Potter boys were hopping mad. It showed in their faces, all smooth except that of the eldest. Bart's left cheek was black and blue, the eye almost swollen shut. His nose was skewed crazily to one side. He'd recently been in a fight—a painful one—and had come out on the losing end.

Damn, but that bastard, Jack Pike, was handy with his fists!

Bart asked Ab, "Was Pike packin' the horn?"

"Naw. Pity you dropped it atter you got yer hands on it."

"I found it in his trap shed, and—"

"Yeah, you told us. Then he came outside on account of he heard you outside his place. The two of you tangled, and you got yer face punched in. And you dropped the horn in the snow. Butterfingers!"

Bart Potter held his knuckles against the frozen ground. His hands—like his whole body—ached ferociously. Going up against Pike barehanded, that had been his big mistake.

Maybe there were more mistakes. "Ab? There's something I got to ask. We appreciate you tellin' on Pike, how you seen him with Paw's horn when you was at his place. But how'd you recognize Clem's carvings?"

"Thought I explained," Walsh lied. "I ran into old Iz last summer. Down Taos way. He was showin' the horn around to all the fellas. Made the old boy proud as a pigeon."

"How do we know for sure that Paw's dead?"

This time Walsh was ready. "Did he keep his ronnyvoo up here with his sons? Is he in Eagle

Valley now?" Ab spat in the snow. "Ask yerself this, Bart. Would old Iz have give up that horn whilst he was alive?"

"Well-l-l, no."

His brother put in, "Hell, no!"

"Paw thought a lot o' the thing. He'd die rather'n see it stole!"

"I rest my case." Walsh knocked back his drink. Then, "Waugh!" The Ludlow's Bay toady belched.

Down the slope from where he and the brothers hunkered, Walsh could see the trappers of Eagle Valley coming and going. Starting out to tend their trap lines. By now the streams were frozen bank to bank, and the snows had left the paths drifted— as much as four feet deep. Across the gulch from Walsh's position loomed a huge white dune.

Walsh kept his eyes fixed there. He was about to tell his biggest lie yet.

"Don't know if I mentioned this before, fellas. I did hear Pike brag on shootin' old Iz down. To that woman of his, Jenny what's-her-name." Ab put an innocent expression on his queer, small face. "It appears your pa got it on his way up here."

"Pike ran into Paw on the trail?"

"That tears it!" Justin Potter jumped to his feet. "We'll take Pike, for sure! Tonight!"

Walsh said lazily, "Why wait? There he walks, yonder. Right now." He pointed. "For some reason hikin' with that Rufus Brumley fella. Looks like bushwhack bait to this coon, by damn!"

Bart's hand drifted to his belt-slung tomahawk. Then he abandoned the hand-ax. But Clem grabbed his forearm, held it in a steely grip. "This is rifle work. Let me stalk the son of a bitch."

148

"They're hikin' in the direction of Long Pond, it looks like," Justin said. "If I recollect, there's an overlook there. Nice spot for an ambush."

"Awright, but prime your gun afresh," Bart, the natural leader of the group, directed. "Then go after the polecat."

"And where, exactly, did you see the big painter cat?" With each word, a puff of vapor came from Pike's mouth. It was cold outside, very cold. Still, the big man was taking this hunt seriously. He knew his quarry was an animal to be reckoned with.

"Long Pond, at the foot of the slope," Rufus Brumley croaked. The young man's face was pale and drawn. His encounter that morning had been with the biggest mountain lion he'd ever imagined.

Since Brumley had come to Pike an hour ago, the wind had grown gusty, chiller. Now ice particles were blowing against the men's faces.

Still, there might be a chance to slay the big killer cat . . .

"He'd robbed three of my traps," Brumley said again. "Like he knew 'zactly what he was doing! Lordy, but he was big!"

"How big?"

"Longer'n a man is tall. 'Bout seven feet from nose to asshole. Color, it's a real light brown, with gray ear tips, muzzle. And them dangerous yeller eyes—Jesus!"

Pike's eyes scanned the white terrain. No catamount could be seen as yet. But Rufus was pointing. "Up ahead is where I set some big traps. For wolverines. Baited with castoreum, on account of wolverines love to eat beaver. But all that was in the traps was chewed-up bones. And then the painter was alookin' me in the eye! Why sure, I hightailed!"

Pike's sharp eyes picked out some tracks. Cat tracks. As the big man knelt to study them, Rufus happened to lift his gaze. Did he catch a gleam of metal up on the ridge? Another hunter, maybe?

Pike was talking. "Cat was here. Long gone, though."

"Yeah?"

All around, the landscape was magnificent. And the ridge was a hundred yards off, at least.

"What's the matter, kid? See something?

"No, Pike. Not a doggone thing worth mention."

Chapter 25

Bart, Clem and Justin Potter seethed with hate. And rage. It was as if acid were burning their bellies, and their minds could only dwell on the thought of revenge—revenge against Jack Pike. They believed Ab Walsh's story, that Pike's possession of the carved powder horn proved he'd killed their pa. It made sense to the brothers. It accounted for the fact that old Iz hadn't met them in the valley as planned.

Of course, Pike had never laid eyes on the horn before that morning. Bart had found it in Pike's shed, but only because *Ab Walsh had planted it.*

But this, the Potter boys couldn't know.

They didn't suspect Walsh of lying. They knew nothing of Ab's deal with LeSage to put Pike out of the way, deprive the free trappers of a leader—both in order to promote a Ludlow's Bay fur monopoly. The view of the Potters had been summed

151

up by Justin, the least stupid: "What's in it for Walsh to fool us?"

Bart and Clem had no answer to that.

So now Clem Potter, chilled to the bone, stalked Pike. So Pike wasn't alone—who cared? Pike could be shot down, even with Rufus Brumley present. Vengeance was all.

As for Ab Walsh, he watched from afar through a battered spyglass. Long ago he'd learned to let others do the dirty work. Through the lens he could see Clem, lugging his rifle, as he scrambled along the ridge. The way lay across a jagged granite massif. The high ground overlooked beaver-rich Long Pond, where, it appeared, Jack Pike was headed.

The idea of an ambush was a good one.

Walsh, at a distance of 300 yards, found a convenient rock shelf. He crammed his mouth with chaw tobacco, sat back to wait. This murder was going to be risk-free—for him.

That was the kind the Arkansan most enjoyed.

Clem Potter made his way along the ridge, which was snow covered. But ahead he saw an even better vantage point: a point farther ahead, in a niche that led up a rock chimney. The grade to the niche wasn't steep, being indented with stairlike depressions.

But he'd need to hurry to reach his position in time.

Down by the frozen pond, Pike had given up kneeling. He and the kid, Rufus, were standing and jawing. Soon they'd be on the move again. Clem relished his chance to avenge his paw, and at the same time grow in his brothers' eyes. He was tired of being the family artist, good for whittling, chiseling, but not truly "manly" exploits.

"God damn you, Pike!"

Clem floundered through a drift, gained the slope, started up. Then things got trickier. Gambling on the footing, slipping at times, he started the next leg of his climb, digging in with each foot carefully.

And then he was at the peak! He flopped down on the stony ground, feeling its cold reach him through his clothes. He rested the barrel of his flintlock across a boulder, checked his sights.

He drew the hammer back. The *click* was loud.

"Come on now, Jack Pike. Just walk into range!"

"Right up ahead, you say? That's where the painter crouched and snarled at you?"

Rufus looked Pike squarely in the eye. "Yeah, there. Alongside that stunted spruce. I was just about to—"

The boom of the rifle cut the winter air, ripping the silence to shreds. Pike, who happened to be looking at Rufus, saw a spectacular display of exploding gore.

The young man's face was incredibly distorted as the nose's bridge caved in. On a downward trajectory, the slug blew the back of Rufus's skull out, scattering shards of bone in a wide arc. Blood-droplets sprayed in a rosy halo. The kid's rifle dropped from limp hands, bouncing on the ground, keeping Rufus company as his dead body folded over.

Pike heard a crunch as the neck snapped like a

bent twig. Simultaneously the mountain man spun, eyes raking the ridge line. A grayish gauze of smoke clouded above a peak. He'd have a minute before the marksman could reload.

Pike bent over the corpse of his young friend. One eye was blown away, the socket leaking crimson on white snow. The big man was sickened, his stomach heaving. Bitter bile choked his throat. But he battled back the nausea, clenched the Hawken in his fist, started running toward the broad, high, rock face.

He had no doubt the shot had been meant for him, a follow-up to last night's attempt. Hatred flooded Jack Pike's brain. He'd get the damned ambusher!

Within seconds he reached the detritus slope and started up.

Clem Potter recharged his weapon and cursed his miss. Pike's companion was dead, but the big man wasn't. *Damn!* He'd spotted Pike raking for the massif, knew it was his turn to be stalked, knew it was time to find himself a dig-in. Fleeing didn't occur to Clem.

He aimed to scalp Pike, present his hair to his brothers, relish their amazement. *Then* they'd have to treat him like a man.

A hunch told Clem to climb some more. Above towered the stone chimney, not an easy go. But it would put him above his pursuer. Allow him to shoot down. He reached up the rock face for a handhold, found it, and hauled himself up along the plane.

As he was going, his moccasined foot dislodged a miniature boulder. Throwing little pebbles and rocks ahead, the boulder went tumbling down. Well, maybe the fall wouldn't give him away.

This time he'd shoot Pike from a much closer distance. Twenty feet? Ten feet?

Clem Potter held crazed laughter in. Damn! This was fun.

Like shooting fish in a barrel.

Chapter 26

As Pike climbed, the slope got tougher, and he found himself panting. By the time he'd gained fifty feet above the valley floor, the game trail he'd been following had petered out. From this point on it would be climbing without any trail at all to follow.

He rested, catching his breath, and watched the air he exhaled emerge in huge, white vapor clouds. He strained his ears to hear any trace of movement in the rocks above. There were no sounds. Silence as deafening as the earlier, shattering gunshot boom lay upon the landscape.

Glancing at the sky, Pike noticed some high-floating cinder specks.

Buzzards, by God!

He found handholds and resumed his climb.

He moved with great care, testing each foothold before relying on it to support his whole weight.

156

Also, he took advantage of each outcrop, trying to stay under cover. He didn't want to get surprised. The way he looked at it, he was vulnerable in three ways: he could be shot at, have a knife thrown at him, or get jumped by a bare-handed attacker. He thought getting shot at was most likely.

Until another notion crossed his mind.

The man up there waiting could easily launch a killer rockslide!

Pike moved even more carefully now, the heavy Hawken eared to half-cock. Thinking he heard something, he pulled up and listened. He peered up at the ridge.

He didn't have much farther to go, and the stretch from his position was not too steep—not so much as what he'd negotiated. But the incline wasn't the worst. The ground ahead was open.

And the crest was at least thirty yards off. Thirty ice-glazed, slippery yards!

But there was no other way. He slung his Hawken over his back by its thong, stood tall from his resting posture. Took a step into the open. After that it was an all-fours scamper, up the rocks to the rim. His passage was almost silent, but in the vast mountain quiet he thought he heard himself.

Cresting the ridge, Pike caught a movement from the corner of his eye. He dropped and rolled, just as Clem Potter rose up and fired. Flame blossomed from the man's rifle, a bee-buzz whine sang in Pike's ear, and his hat sailed off. The slug slammed the rock wall near Pike's head, tiny granite chips ripping his cheek.

Now he was mad as hell.

He triggered the Hawken.

He, too, missed.

Yelping, Clem dodged in back of a boulder and fled. Pike scrambled after the bushwhacker. Clearing the boulder himself, he saw his foe race down a footpath. As Pike watched, the man tripped and fell headfirst. His mouth opened, and he roared out: "Murderer! My paw, he was just a harmless old coot!"

As Pike charged up, his enemy pulled a knife and lunged. But Pike brought his Kentucky pistol to bear. The big man fired, and the gun spat flame and hot lead.

Clem, whose name Pike didn't even know, took the ball. He threw up his hands as his body spasmed. The knife spun away, and Clem performed a grotesque dance, jerking, whirling on stiffening legs. The pain in his slug-chewed liver was unendurable.

The sounds the man bawled were horrible. Dying cries. His breath whistled in and out. He was puking green bile. Pike rushed close, but the man stepped off the lip of the gorge, careening into space. He windmilled all the way down, 300 feet, at least. Went headfirst into the snow packed in the gorge's bottom.

Buried there, the body was lost till spring. Perhaps lost forever. Those rock walls were almost perpendicular.

Pike stood bareheaded on the windy ridge crest. The wind rippled his brown hair and beard. What in hell was he to think? He'd just trounced another attacker, one who'd been a stranger to him.

And what was it the man had yelled? Some nonsense about a father.

Could he—Pike—have known the gent's father? To hell with it!

The temperature was definitely dropping. Tiny flakes dropped from the sky, but they weren't wind-borne. They fell straight from the low, gray cloud cover.

If the sky cleared, the temperature would plummet. Conditions were good for small animals to make thick furs.

Not so good for a booshway beset with mysteries.

Chapter 27

"All right, let me get it straight. You killed the jasper, and the body went into the ravine. But before that, you got a good look at him?"

"He was in his twenties," Pike told Skins, both mountain men working furs outside McConnell's lodge. "Nothing unusual about the face. I didn't recognize it."

"But the face wasn't bruised? The man hadn't been in a fight lately?"

Pike shook his head. "No. He wasn't the same one as jumped me, night before last."

"Puzzling."

McConnell, using his skinning knife, cut into a beaver carcass and peeled back the skin. With care he hung the raw pelts on a tree limb. Then he picked up and flexed a willow drying hoop. "Don't make no sense," he opined. "Claimed you murdered his pap? Who'd you kill in the last year, Jack? Anybody who'd fill the bill?"

"Naw." Pike sliced off a beaver's tail. The delicacy would make good eating, a taste resembling pig meat. "And another thing." Now he was scraping a pelt, a prime one he'd put to stretch yesterday—removing every scrap of fat. "The two who tried to kill me—and *did* kill Rufus—were they in cahoots?"

"Seems likely," McConnell agreed. Then he looked sidelong at his pard and grinned. "Seems you're a gent with enemies, Jack. Expect more to come at you outa the underbrush?"

Pike winked. "Can't say, but I'll be watching my back. That's something now."

"You do that, Jack. You do that."

In the midst of the wind-blocking stand of junipers the dozen men stood. All were shrouded in bear- or wolfhide capotes, all were bearded, squint-eyed, mean-faced. Each clutched a heavy Kentucky rifle.

The angriest of the bunch were the Potter boys, Bart and Justin. Ab Walsh had just informed them of their brother's fate. Now the cold urine-hued eyes flashed hate.

"You sat there, ass on a cold rock, and let it happen? Watched Pike kill Clem! Walsh, you're no-good scum!"

The Ludlow's Bay man gave a wicked smile. "I'll pardon your talkin' riled this once. Seein' as how your kin's recent kilt. Remember, Pike pulled the trigger, not me."

"He's right, Bart," Justin said. "Ab was too far away. Beyond rifle range. He couldn't have picked Pike off. And we'd told him 'twas to be Clem's play."

Some of the other men shuffled moccasin soles. "Yeah, Bart. Lay off Ab."

"Ab's awright."

"Figures to make us all rich."

"Sure as beaver plews are called 'soft gold.' "

Walsh drew himself up to full height. Wagged his meaty shoulders. "Now for the reason I called y'all—my crew—together! It's like this. The big snow, she's sure to come in the next few days!"

"What we been waitin' for, ain't it, Ab? Soon as the pass is drifted shut, we move agin th' hard-workin' fools! Make their furs our furs!"

"What the hell's a bit o' bloodshed?"

Walsh spun to face the speaker. "By God, you're c'rect, Cold Chuck Johnny! And don't the rest of you feel the same?"

Some men bobbed their chins, some spat tobacco juice. All murmured in agreement. Except one.

Bart Potter spoke up gruffly. "Oh, you talk big, Ab Walsh. About us bad-asses rulin' the valley. Grabbin' the pelts. Them trappers as fight back, we shoot. But how do we be sure Ludlow's Bay will treat us fair?" To the group, he questioned, "Baptiste LeSage gave his word? His word to Ab? Phooey! Hell, Ab's a man can't stand up to Jack Pike! Needs us t'do his dirty work! *I* say let's vote in another leader! *I* say—"

Walsh butted in, his voice rough as flint. "Hey, you snot-nosed punk! Shut up in front of your betters! Here's a lesson!" The man's tomahawk came

162

out and up. Was thrust under Bart Potter's nose. The iron felt icy.

"Dub? Burl? Grab th' loudmouth pipsqueak!"

Instantly Bart's arms were pinned.

"Ya can't do this," he rasped.

"Oh, no?"

The blade of the razor-sharp tool flashed. A square of skin was parted from Bart's upper lip. The painful shallow wound oozed blood.

"Here's more!" The tomahawk fell again. Slammed Bart's front teeth. Knocked one out, snapped the other off. "Now, Bart. Who runs this outfit?"

"You, Ab! You!"

"Again?"

"You, Ab!"

"Sound like he means it, boys?"

"We dunno—"

"Me neither. So, Bart, take this!" Walsh's foot pumped high, burying in Bart's gut. The young man hinged double. The hand-ax's haft crashed to his head. He sprawled in the snow.

Walsh confronted Justin. "Any gripes 'bout what happened?"

"To my brother? Er, no, Ab. No."

"Good kid." Walsh's free hand rumpled the kid's scant chinwhiskers. "Now, we got work to do, hear? Get rich and revenge your paw. Only thing standing in our way's Jack Pike!

"And the son of a bitch's days, ain't they numbered, though!"

Chapter 28

The fire roared merrily in Pike's hearth, even though the mountain man was out of the cabin. Jenny was out too, gone to check the mink trap she'd set with a view to catching something and surprising Jack. Only Flo was at home, and the comely young woman was so drowsy that her eyelids kept fluttering shut.

She'd been up most of the night, as usual, and now sat cross-legged on the floor, relaxing and thinking. In the spring she'd be Oregon bound, for sure. Nothing was going to prevent this move to get her life back on track.

She could picture the blooming apple trees all up and down the valley of the Wilamette. There'd be towns with real churches and schools. Maybe she'd turn schoolmarm. She'd taken training along that line, long ago, back East. That was before her life had turned more stinking than dog turds ...

Now she heard a faint noise outside. Her day-dream evaporated in a flash.

Someone threw back the hide door-flap, crowded inside, backside first.

"Pike, is that you? Jenny? Say, how cold *is* it out-side? That great big scarf wound across your face—"

The man whipped away the scarf, uncovering his features. He was a total stranger to the woman. Surprisingly, Flo thought him interesting-looking, with his pixyish face and dark, bright eyes. She gave him a smile that wasn't merely pasted on. "Well, now! Howdy, mister!"

Ab Walsh scowled angrily. "Where's Jenny Henderson? I come t'see that bitch!"

"Bitch? Now, just a minute, you—"

The big-shouldered man loomed over the dimin-utive woman. He grabbed the front of her wool shirt, almost popping buttons. "I'll call her what I want! So, when'll she be back?"

"I won't tell you! So, get out, or I'll scream!"

"Don't even *think* of pipin' out a squawk. See this?"

Whether this sorrel-haired, petite woman screamed made little difference to Walsh. The cabin lay in an isolated draw. Jack Pike was a mile away, clear over at the red-niggers' village.

Walsh pulled his knife, which gleamed in the firelight.

Flo gasped. "Is that human hair, sewn to the haft?" Her heart beat fast. Was it fear or lust? She couldn't always tell . . .

"I can see the kind of guy you are, mister. But listen, I can take care of you better than ol' Jen. Even if you like doin' it rough, I ain't unwilling. I can stand a whale of a lot—"

165

This man she stood looking at moved with animal grace. In the whole valley, only two might be his equal. But Jack Pike was already taken by Jenny, and Skins McConnell was shacked up with a pretty squaw. Although there'd been a time when she'd had a chance at Skins, she'd thought herself unworthy.

The time she'd been gang-raped by brigade men . . . She'd felt so dirty . . . Only recently had she managed to come back to life . . .

"Mister? Lets jump in the bedroll. We'll talk about money later. Here, let me show—"

She tugged open the shirt, releasing her breasts. Big, elongated, melon breasts. Firm, proud breasts . . .

This wasn't what the Arkansan wanted, not now. Jenny wasn't here, Pike wasn't here. He'd have to work at killing them another time. Another time, but they mustn't have a word of warning.

Wouldn't this slut wriggling her ass for him warn Jenny and Pike? Pass on his description?

"C'mon, mister. I'll just shuck my britches—"

"Bare skin, it makes it easy for me!" Walsh drove the six-inch blade of steel under Flo's short ribs. Her eyes bugged wide in surprise.

Her mouth formed a soundless O.

Walsh's fist slammed her voice box, bursting it. The woman shuddered from top to toe, collapsed. Thudded to the floor, stone dead.

There'd be no tales to tell on him now, thought Walsh. He'd leave unseen, just the way he'd come. He'd take care to sweep out his footprints with a leafy branch.

He'd killed for expediency this time, not vengeance, but tomorrow was another day.

Outside by now, the snow was falling in soft flakes the size of dollar coins.

"Pike! Pike!" The words through the white swirl had a spooky, unearthly ring. Now that it had been snowing in the valley for an hour, visibility was bad—very bad. At the voice, Pike let go the trap he'd been holding, bringing his rifle up and around smoothly. He squinted to see the arrival.

McConnell stepped to his side. "Jack, it's Jenny! And she looks like hell!"

The woman was slogging ahead determinedly through knee-deep, powdery white stuff. She was ear-deep in her warmest coat, and her face was pale as if she'd seen a ghost—or worse. "Jesus, Pike," she wailed sobbingly. "I was out of the cabin, down by the pond—I'll tell you why sometime—and when I got back, I found—"

"Don't stop talking, gal. *What* did you find?"

"Flo! Or rather, Flo's body! She's dead! It was so horrible!" A cough and a wheeze, and then Jenny could go on. "Flo'd been stabbed in the chest, oh so many times! Lord, her whole left breast's cut to ribbons!"

"Let's go. Show us."

The men and woman fell in line, Pike leading, and found the going not too hard, Jenny having broken the drifts. Rounding the familiar loaf-shaped hill, they came in sight of the cabin, a snowcapped bedraggled structure. Jenny was repeating her story of finding her friend's corpse, when Pike raised his hand to cut her off. "Skins and I, we'll move in on the place, Jenny. Each

167

from a different angle. Could be the killer's come back."

"Why would he come back?"

"He probably hasn't. The whole thing's iffy as hell. But, for sure, we oughtta be safe, not sorry."

"I see now, Pike," the woman admitted.

"I figured you'd see it my way."

Then it was McConnell's turn to butt in. "Jack! In among those spruce yonder! Movement!"

Pike dropped into an alert crouch, and his voice became a low hiss. "Jenny, wait here. Skins, you take the left approach to the stand; me, I'll go around, come at him from the other way. Have your rifle cocked as you move in. Don't fool with whoever's in there—if he's killed once, he'll kill again."

The men parted, each breaking through deeper and deeper snow cover. The dark evergreens stood like motionless sentinels.

It was McConnell who flushed out the one who'd taken refuge. The smallish figure in buckskins started running as best he could, legs punching through white surface crust, falling, then jumping up and floundering on again. Pike raced to head him off, tripped in the virgin snow, but managed to thrust the Hawken at arm's length overhead, keeping the weapon's powder dry. Finally Pike simply yelled, "Freeze, else I'll ventilate you!"

The kid stopped in his tracks, flung his hands up, turned to face the ones having the drop.

"Who the hell are you?" All the big man could see was the obvious: the ten-year-old was a full-blooded Snake. Pike didn't, in fact, recall ever having taken notice of him.

"I'll tell you who he is!" Skins said. He puffed as

he stamped up. "Jack, meet Brown Turtle, brother to Summer Rain. You remember Summer Rain. Damn it, this 'un don't look mean enough to skewer a full-grown woman."

The kid piped up in a shrill, high voice. "Me, I kill nobody! But I see a white man go to the cabin. After a while, he comes out and walks off. Later, when I peek in the door, I see the flame-haired woman on the floor. She not move. Lots of blood down her front." By this time Brown Turtle grew bold. "I'm thinking this white man, he's a bad man!"

"So, who was the son of a bitch? You seen him before? If so, where?"

"Hell, Jack, Brown Turtle, he prob'ly doesn't know the trappers' handles. Best ask what the killer looked like. How about it, kid? Was he tall? Short? Middle-size?"

"Brown Turtle know this man. Live in the camp, see him all time. Kick and cuss the little Snake braves—me and friends. Is the one called Walsh! The man who killed the woman, he is Walsh!"

"Christ!" McConnell blurted.

"I might've expected something like this," Pike snapped, his face a mask of barely suppressed fury. The eyes were fever-bright, and flicked from side to side. The massive hand clenched and unclenched the frame of the Hawken.

Of course, if he'd killed Walsh days ago, Flo would be alive now. And if Walsh hadn't tried twice to kill Jack Pike, he'd tricked some shithead fool into trying for him. *Goddamn you, Ab Walsh!*

"Skins, go fetch Jenny to the main camp. Brown Turtle, you run and pass the word to your tribe's head men. I want to meet with 'em. Myself, I'll saddle the bay, go and round up some of the best coons in the valley. Elijah and Gap-Tooth. Joe Slocum, Whiskey Sam and the rest. He might have sidekicks, so we'll get us up a posse."

"What if Walsh lights a shuck?" McConnell asked. "Rides straight on up out of the valley? Do we chase him over the mountains?"

"Oh, I don't guess he'll leave the valley," Pike stated flatly. "Look!" A wide arm wave took in the sky. The sun was blotted out, and there was no blue up there: nothing but stinging, wind-driven snow. The first fluffy flakes had changed, and were now the small, grainy particles that rode harsh storm weather.

An ominous chill lay in the air. The farther mountain peaks couldn't be seen. Wind-rippled waves of white were spread across the valley floor. High drifts rose like redoubts in the middle distance.

"Remember the lay of the pass? A narrow gap the wind'll eddy through. Dropping the snow it carries, drifting twenty or thirty feet deep!"

"Then, it's too late for Walsh to get across?"

"You said it all just then, Skins. The bastard killed here, and he'll die here. Now, let's get that posse organized and take him."

Chapter 29

"Where'd the bastards clear off to, d'ya suppose?"

"Besides Walsh, they's a bunch more gone from the main camp. All three Potter boys, plus Dub Perkins, Burl Meese."

"Them's just the ones we know 'bout, Pike. Could be more missing. A passel more!"

The trappers were gathered in front of the fire in Pike's cabin, from which the remains of Flo Lipscomb had been tenderly carried. Now the body lay out back in the fur shed, awaiting the thaw of the ground next spring, when it could be buried. The fire was hot, and so were the feelings. Pike and McConnell were madder than wing-torn hornets over the valley deaths, both Flo's and Rufus Brumley's. The other mountain men were hardly less so.

McConnell summed up the meat of the discussion. "So everything points to Walsh having organized a gang. What can he be up to? Kill Jack Pike, sure—but *only* kill Jack Pike?"

Beard wagging and droopy eyelids twitching, ancient Whiskey Sam Benedict broke wind—and silence. "I'd say sure, there be more behind it! Just like there's more to killin' Jack than gettin' even. So Jenny ditched Ab. Shit, lots o' gals dump assholes."

"True," Elijah Rowe grouched. "Too true."

"I'll say this! The bastards gotta be caught! Killing's no good, but neither's thieving!" The man who'd jumped to his feet was Badger McGrew, unwashed but vehement. "T'day I spied inside m' cache o' plews. Half of 'em gone, I swear! Stole! Coulda been Walsh and his crew."

"No proof 'o that, Badger," said Gap-Tooth.

"No proof them polecats be innocent!"

"What's the scouts say? *They've* had their eyes open. Injuns allus do!"

"Black Feather, the subchief, he's calling in his braves. He'll be ready to ride, come sunup, like us!"

"Then watch out, Ab Walsh—we got our lynch rope measured and bear-greased! First we lift his topknot, then string the sidewinder up!"

"I plan to bring 'em back alive, so's to put 'em on trial" said Pike firmly. "We're a posse, not a mob."

"He's right," Skins McConnell affirmed.

The coffee was low in the pot when Pike adjourned, the trappers stamped out into the night. The weather hadn't let up, but Pike hoped it might by morning. The honest trappers all vowed they'd keep their fingers crossed.

McConnell was the last to leave. From the door flap he looked down at wide, dark bloodstains that

172

dyed the floor. "A damned shame she's gone. Flo was a good woman. Just mixed up."

"Amen," said Jenny.

"Amen," said Pike.

Then Skins was out the door, and the couple was alone together. They peered into each other's eyes, and the heat between them started stoking. Jen put her small hand in Jack Pike's huge one. Squeezed. "Bedroll?"

"Bedroll."

He swept her up in his arms and carried her. Deposited the woman on the piled buffalo robes. She wriggled swiftly out of her clothes. "Skin to skin, Pike! Christ, but I need you tonight. Hurry!"

Immediately his flesh responded to her flesh. With her curvaceous, cream-smooth body pressed close, his penis grew to barber-pole dimensions. His hands cupped her large, pillowing breasts.

"It's Flo who's dead, not us, Pike. It's our need now to affirm life!"

"Tell me about it!"

Jenny's melodic laughter filled the place. "Making you feel it, that's best of all! Take this, you great hunk of man-meat!"

Sudden shivers of desire racked the man and woman, and the couple melted against each other. Her fingers splayed across his massive chest, his palm cupped her bush-thatched come-together. Jenny squirmed as his thumb explored her treasure cove, at the same time she milked his swollen plum. Heaving on top of Pike, she sat astride his groin, the shaft of him poised under her.

"Here goes!"

Her hot wetness accepted his cock.
Paradise closed in.

In the morning Pike slipped from the bedroll, and while Jenny still slept, tiptoed and raised the frost-stiff door flap. He peered out at the new day. It felt cold inside, but out there it was colder. Needles stung the big man's lungs when he inhaled.

He saw soft, wet snow mounding high up the door, and away from the cabin the clearing had been blown level full. The wind roared about the eaves, causing all four walls to tremble. What appeared of the sun was wan, coming and going as curtains of snow rushed past its face. In every direction Pike looked, he saw nothing but hills of winter white.

"Jesus!"

From the buffalo robes, Jenny called, "Pike? You say something?"

Sliding back under and against her, he said, "I'm not going anywhere today. Nobody in the valley is."

"Blizzard?"

"Big one. Can't say when it'll let up."

"Happy where you are?"

His enormous sausage nudged her cleft.

She cooed. "Yes! That's how I like it! Hmmm-mmmm!"

They bucked, romped, and kept themselves warm.

Part Three
The Snow

Chapter 30

The winter storm that tore through Eagle Valley and the surrounding Bitterroots was the real thing. For three long days the thick snowflakes swirled in a blinding curtain. The weather turned cold, then more cold. All the world turned winter white, every trail was packed with sculptured snow dunes. Winds blew harshly down from the north, cycloning across open stretches, eddying under snow-laden woods, filtering into every canyon.

By the fifth day the temperature had dropped to twenty below zero. It was a world of jewel-crusted mesas of snow and ice. There was beauty, but danger, too: trees split open with cannoning *cracks*; horses keeled over where they stood, and as soon as they were on the ground, froze to death. The cold was such that it would weld a person's fingers to the iron of a gun, if one were careless.

Streams and ponds were solid to their bottoms,

and trapping was impossible. The mountain men—Pike and the rest—kept to themselves, holed up. The Snake Indians remained in their lodges.

There wasn't a manhunt because there *couldn't* be a manhunt.

On the sixth day, the cold finally broke. When Pike ventured out for firewood that morning, his greased face felt a trace of a mild chinook breeze. Pike strapped on willow-bow snowshoes strung with rawhide mesh, hiked over to McConnell's branch-and-earth shelter.

Coming up on the tied-shut door, Pike grinned at the sounds he heard from the cramped interior.

"Ah-aaah!" crooned a woman's voice. "Ah-ah-aaah!" A thump ensued, then several minutes' silence.

"Er . . . Skins?" the big man called.

After a long moment's delay, "Yo?"

"It's Pike standing out here. By any chance you through doing what you were doing?"

"Me and Summer Rain? Yeah, we finished a minute ago."

"Well, if it isn't too much trouble, come stick your head out and take a look around. The weather's a lot better today."

McConnell's sleepy-eyed face thrust out, surrounded with matted hair above, a matted beard below. A grin spread slowly across his features. "No more being cooped up? Hot damn! Jack, just wait'll I pull on my pants and cold-weather mocs. I'll be right out!"

Shortly afterward, Pike and McConnell were trudging across the white crust toward Gap-Tooth's and Elijah's adjoining huts. "Skins," Pike told his

178

pard, "you figure you missed your calling, should've gone into the theater? What was that a minute ago but a big act, letting on you were tired of being with Summer Rain?"

"You know how it is, Jack. Of course I'm not tired of her. But it never did any harm, letting a woman think you're on the verge of getting fed up. Tends to keep her eager to please—and her loving hot."

"Oh, really?"

"Come on now, Jack. Don't try and tell me you've never done the same?"

"Haven't needed to, Skins. I reckon *my* women stay naturally eager to please, on account of me just being me."

"Ah, but you're Mountain Jack Pike, weighing in at—what you weigh in at. With the reputation of being He-Whose-Head-Touches-the-Sky. In other words, being God's gift to the female sex!"

"You make it seem rough, being plain, ordinary Skins McConnell."

"Oh, it isn't too rough, Jack. Not at all. I've had my share of willing, hot women over the years. My only wish is, I'd met the needs of some of 'em better."

Pike's snowshoe slipped on a patch of ice. When he regained his balance he frowned and said, "Skins, you can't feel guilty about what happened to Flo. You couldn't have prevented it. Those last months before she was killed, she did exactly what she wanted."

Skins gritted his teeth. "Christ, that she had to've gone that way! Cut up by that sidewinder Walsh. Jack, we've got to bring him in—or shoot him down like a coyote!"

"That's what we're tending to now, Skins. Get the trappers together, lay out manhunt plans."

"Jack, you sure he can't have gotten out of the valley? Him and his sidekicks?"

Pike answered with an arm wave. "Just look at all that snow." In all directions, as far as the eye could see, the frozen beauty stretched. The enormous drifts glittered in the sunlight like jewels, but certainly choked every pass in or out of the valley.

"Yeah, Walsh still has to be here. Maybe when we get out riding, he'll ride into our gunsights."

"We can hope, Skins. We can hope."

Pike stood tall atop a flat-topped stump, looking out over the forest of upturned mountain men's faces. The days of idleness and rest had made them more eager to corral Ab Walsh—and any sidekicks that could be rounded up. But Jack Pike didn't want a lynching. "If we can, we'll bring him and his crew in, give 'em a trial, and eventually hang 'em proper! I want you fellas to agree to that! Now, all in favor, holler aye!"

A chorus of ayes went up.

Just when the cheers were echoing, a gunshot sounded from back behind Pike's cabin. Pike paid no attention, but went on with his speech. "I've thought long and hard, and I think I've come up with the best plan! You're going to hear it now, and if any of you has questions, raise 'em! I aim to divide the valley up, send men to each flat, stream gully, blind canyon! You boys are going to look high and low!"

180

Another booming report rang out, from the same Kentucky rifle as before. Again, Pike ignored it. "A top mountain man will ride at the head of each of the small posses! Gap-Tooth Williams's bunch will take the north end. Elijah Rowe's will canvas the south. Joe Mahony, the ponds out east. Phil Lee the central bottoms. And each band'll take along a handful of Black Feather's Snake braves! They're damned fine trackers and scouts!"

A gruff-voiced man raised a question. "I got somethin' to ask!"

"Let's hear it."

"About the killers of Flo Lipscomb and Rufus Brumley. You said no scalpin' of the bastards if'n we take 'em alive. What if'n we take 'em dead?"

Pike considered a moment, then said, "A mountain man's gotta do what a mountain man's gotta do."

Another shot, the third in five minutes, rang out. However Pike was winding down the meeting. "All right, men, go to your horses and mount up. Skins McConnell and I and an Indian called Blue Hand—Black Feather's nephew—will make up the last party. Oh, and one other rider! We'll be covering the west end of the valley. Sure, it's rough country; that's why I'm going along to be the leader!"

"Who's yore fourth person?" Badger McGrew piped up.

At that moment, Jenny Henderson appeared on the cabin path. She strode forward with a distinct swagger, dressed warmly for winter riding. The seams of her buckskins were stitched tightly, with

181

long fringes down the arms and legs, around the bottom of the shirt. She wore thick wolverineskin boots over her moccasins, a heavy wolfskin coat.

"Here she is now," Pike announced. Already McConnell was loading himself with rifle, powder horns, and shot pouch as he moved toward his saddled chestnut. The woman stepped to Pike's side. "How'd your target practice go, Jenny?"

"All the old skill's come back. I'm ready as I'm going to be." She slapped the knife and tomahawk at her belt. Then softly, so that none except Pike could hear, "Thanks for letting me come. Flo was my friend, and I hate Ab Walsh!"

Pike roared to the men, "All right, let's ride!" The shouted words rang with mighty lung power. "We'll meet back here in three days, if not sooner! And may the best and luckiest of us come up against Ab Walsh!"

Chapter 31

Under a bright sky, but through monumental, gleaming snowdrifts, Jack Pike and his party gigged their mounts along. The crust was unbroken, the white stuff very deep everywhere. The mounts waded, rather than walked, and had to be allowed often to rest.

Within the first five miles of following a frozen beaver stream, the cold began to get to Pike, McConnell, Blue Hand and Jenny. The woman couldn't feel her toes, and her arms seemed leaden. And the men weren't too comfortable riding, either: their faces reddened by the cold and the exertion.

They floundered into drift snow higher than a man's head, and had to backtrack, detour around the deepest part. From a mile away across a flat they spotted a strange black dot, and rode straight toward it. As they approached it, they reined in,

Blue Hand raising his hand with a shout. "Look, He-Whose-Head-Touches-the-Sky!"

It was an elk, shaggy coated and grotesquely sprawled in death. Half-buried in snow, it lay with neck twisted and outstretched, a position impossible for a living creature. Contorted lips were pulled back, revealing yellow teeth. The animal's muzzle, mouth, and eyes were ice-crusted.

"Frozen," announced the brave.

"My God," Jenny blurted.

"A handsome critter—once," McConnell said.

"Not any more," Pike stated flatly. "Didn't get down out of the high country in time."

They rode up into the high forest, and the trees closed in. They rode low to their mounts' necks, but continued to brush snow-laden branches. The horses picked their way carefully.

They had to avoid the areas of the deepest snow. Ranging up to thirty feet in depth, the whiteness lay flat or mounded, having nothing to do with the lay of the ground beneath. What looked like tiny fir trees were really huge trees, buried to their tips.

Above, the clouds had a thin look, and were blowing east. They heralded no weather change. The snow supported Pike's horse's weight, until joltingly, the stud broke through the crust. The animal took four or five more steps, but then broke through again, going to its knees. It got up, snorting in fright, one foreleg bloodied from ice cuts.

"He'll be all right. We've got to keep going!"

At a point where a deep cut led left, the way narrowed between slick, ice-glazed walls. The party dismounted to lead the horses. And then they rounded a house-sized boulder jumble, and the view opened. Blue Hand's eyes were sharp, but it was Pike who caught sight of the dark smudges under a tall cliff's beetling, snow-piled brow.

Pike reined in his stud.

"What's yonder?" Jenny asked.

"Caves."

McConnell scratched his chin, considering. "Caves make good shelters. You reckon Walsh and his pards waited out the blizzard in there?"

Pike nodded. "Could've. Might still be around, in fact. Can't find out if we don't take a look-see."

"Steep," Blue Hand pointed out. "Horses cannot climb up."

"Then we tie 'em here and scale the grade on snowshoes."

A half hour later and they still hadn't reached the caves. Jenny was glad they'd all brought snowshoes. Now she slogged along behind Pike, who was breaking through the drifts, toiling hard. She could feel the effort in the long muscles of her calves and thighs. Chilblains pained her heels.

Ahead of her, Pike hiked on tirelessly. "How you doing?" he called back at her.

"Fine."

"Rifle's not too heavy?"

"No."

"We're almost there. Just thirty more yards or so."

Jenny smiled at Pike, McConnell, and Blue Hand. Beyond a series of treacherous switchbacks, they could see a dark cavern mouth, opening off a ledge of stone. Spilled rocks from up top headed at the entrance. Back in the cave's depths, little could be seen but inky blackness.

"No tracks to be seen," McConnell said. "Looks like nobody's around."

"No guesswork," Pike said. "Spread out, my friends. We're going in."

Without warning, a gruff, stern voice roared out, "I don't think so!" The voice was accompanied by rolling echoes, loud and bell-toned. Their source, of course, was the cavern.

Ab Walsh stepped into view, his sinister little face set, the yellowish eyes staring bleakly. The rifle of the Ludlow's Bay man was aimed at Pike's forehead. To Walsh's left and right more men showed themselves. Pike recognized two of the Potter brothers and several others. Guns were also pointed at McConnell, Blue Hand, and Jenny.

McConnell felt the gooseflesh standing on his skin. The danger was so real, he could almost smell it. He glanced to either side; saw Blue Hand's face was expressionless, Jenny's was pale. Pike's visage was wreathed in a defiant scowl.

"Drop your guns!" bellowed Walsh.

"In the snow? That'll—"

"Get the powder wet? Fine with me! Just follow orders, Pike! Else you all are dead right where you stand!"

Having no other choice, the four tossed their firearms.

"Now come into the cave, Pike. It's our hideout, you guessed right on that. We been keepin' plumb cozy." Walsh's grin was more than wicked, it was deadly.

Pike's eyes went murky. The big man's hand drifted toward his sheathed skinning knife.

Walsh danced close, rammed his rifle's muzzle

186

into Pike's crotch. "Don't make a move! Don't even blink! Else your balls get blowed to Kingdom Come!" Then to Jenny, "You wouldn't want to see that, would you, former gal-of-mine?"

No, Jenny didn't want to see that. She gritted her teeth, and let herself be shoved forward, stumbling.

"Hands in the air, all of you!"

The four were marched toward the cave's mouth, covered by guns every step of the way.

From what the captives could see beyond the entrance, the cavern's depths were dark as any grave.

Chapter 32

"Halt right there," Ab Walsh barked. "That's far enough, the four of you. Now, stand stock still, where each of you be, whilst the boys run their hands over the outside of your clothes." With a hand, he scrubbed the side of his small head. "I figure yer carryin' hideout weapons. We get rid o' them, we can start havin' fun, Injun-style."

A half dozen men backed Walsh's play, while three men advanced to conduct the searches of the prisoners. The others kept their flintlocks steady, fingers on the triggers. Jack Pike, who was still covered by Ab's rifle, stared unfalteringly into the barrel's large-bore eye.

"What do you mean, Walsh, fun Injun-style?" Pike's voice grated like a carpenter's rasp. "You don't mean torture?"

"Sure, torture! You, Pike. The gal. McConnell and that there Snake redskin! Jen, she left me and run off, and a month later I find her sharin' a bed with Jack Pike! Ya both gotta pay! As for them two—" He indicated Skins and Blue Hand. "Ain't they the unlucky ones? They rode alongside you, Pike. So, y'see, they gotta die painful, too."

Pike found the cavern deeper than expected—so deep that his gaze failed, back in the gloom. After entering the cave he and the others stood under a ceiling thirty feet high. Looking around, Pike saw off to one side a smaller cave, the depths of that one equally gloomy.

An escape route?

Pike sensed a chance to turn the tables, dash into the dark, then come at the jaspers, despite the guns they held. Each firearm held only one charge, and in close fighting, guns weren't the weapons of choice.

Of more use were tomahawks, knives, clubs—even tools like the double-bitted ax he'd glimpsed leaning against the limestone wall. The tool had been used to chop wood for the fire, now extinguished, six feet back from the entrance.

Pike could picture the tool in his hands—putting it to deadly use against Walsh and company.

"How 'bout it, boys," Ab said to his henchmen. "How'll we start out? Build a fire and scorch their hides? Skewer Pike's pecker and the gal's tits, then, whilst they're still alive and screaming, chop 'em into wolf meat?"

The time was coming for Pike to make his move. The mountain man's eyes darted from one foe to another. The weakest in the row of gunmen might be the skinniest—a chinless kid with peach-fuzz whiskers.

But before Pike could spring, hell broke loose! Blue Hand vented a high-pitched whoop, grabbed the nearest foe and snatched him from his feet, bodily. He held the man above his head in both hands, shook him twice, then threw him. The flying jasper bowled down three companions.

Walsh was grinning one minute, and the next his face twisted with savagery. "Blast the damn fools!" he sang out.

Rifles boomed in a ragged fusillade.

In the confines of the cave, the noise was thunderous. The reverberations swelled, went on and on. The cave filled with swirling smoke. Pike heard a rifle ball zip past his ear, then through the acrid haze saw Blue Hand drop to his knees, his eyes bulging. Blood sheeted down his chest, which had been pierced by a half ounce of lead that had torn through, shattering his spine. The Indian teetered for a split second, then pitched to the rock floor. The *plop* was like that of a burst grain sack.

Pike, galvanized into action, dodged in one direction, Skins in another.

Jenny ran for the ax, plucked it up, then scurried into the cave's dark depths.

It was a melee of men battling with hands, knives, any weapon. One jasper raised a cast-iron Dutch oven, hurled it at Pike. Luckily, it missed. Pike, scanning about for Walsh, saw the bastard slugging toe-to-toe with Skins. As the two traded punches, Pike surged through the chaos toward them.

But he found his way blocked. "Grab th' big 'un!" a man yelled.

"Stop him!"

"Brain th' sumbitch!"

One assailant brought up a cocked Kentucky pistol. Pike drove hard knuckles into the gunman's face, knocking aside the weapon. As the man went down, the gun skittered outside, into a snowbank.

"Goddamn!"

Pike waded into the fray, eyes blazing, lips a grim line. But then someone landed on his back, two vicious fists pummeled his head. Pike spun, arching his back, and his attacker was thrown to the ground. He recognized him as a trapper whose name he didn't know. He dove after the man, but Bart Potter's fist sledged toward his face. Pike couldn't get his forearm up.

The blow caught him in the jaw. An explosion went off in his skull.

He staggered and started to go down . . .

Skins McConnell had his hands full. He'd thought he had Walsh cornered, but the sidewinder slipped from his grip and vanished. Now two giants had him crowded to the cave wall. He landed a left uppercut that lifted one inches from the ground. As the jasper reeled back and fell, Skins took on the other, Cold-Chuck Johnny. He drove his left fist into the jasper's gut. As Levitt jackknifed, clutching his belly, McConnell kneed him in the face, and he went down all the way.

A man appeared from nowhere and made a grab, but McConnell raised his leg, pumped a heel to his chest, flinging him back. Then Walsh gave forth a roar, leaping toward Skins. "Here, boys," he bellowed. A moment later, no less than three attackers converged on McConnell.

* * *

Jack Pike scrambled to his feet, battered but brimming with rage. As soon as he put an enemy down, two more seemed to take his place. Now he twisted sideways, trying to elude a man with arms outstretched. But the attacker managed to close, fingers closed around Pike's neck. The pressure there built. A dark shape seemed to clog Pike's brain, his ears rang. Breath whistled through Pike's teeth, he felt unconsciousness gaining on him.

He couldn't live if he couldn't break this enemy's grip. Jenny stalked the man with the choke hold. "Pike!"

The mountain man barely heard her.

Jenny swung the ax she'd appropriated. Heard the hickory handle impact skull. Pike, swearing, twisted free. With a foot, he caught the next attacker in the kneecap. The burly fellow reeled, and Pike threw two sledging blows to the man's kidneys.

Chapter 33

The fight was going bad for McConnell. He wasn't ready to absorb Burl Meese's jab. He deflected his attacker's wrist, but then Ab Walsh suddenly loomed, wading in with both fists swinging. As Ab drew back his right arm, Skins feinted with his left. He put all of his considerable might into an uppercut. But as Ab's head flew back, Justin Potter ran at Skins from behind. While Skins was battering Walsh, the kid brought both clenched fists crashing down. The back of Skins's neck took the blow.

McConnell turned on shaky pins. Grabbed Justin. The kid grunted and pumped his elbows backward, ramming them to McConnell's ribs, breaking his hold. At the same time someone else swung a rifle by its barrel. The walnut stock of the weapon impacted the side of Skins's head, and the mountain man reeled as if poleaxed.

Then they were all over him, their exact number

Skins didn't know and couldn't see. And every one of the gang was clubbing him, kicking him viciously.

"Grizzly" Conroy had Jenny cornered—between a rock and a hard place. Behind her were the dark labyrinths of the cave. To her front stood the buck-skin-clad man with slobbering mouth and lust-crazed eyes.

She had no doubt what he wanted—he had the strength and will to rape her to death. But that wasn't going to happen if Jenny Henderson could help it!

She'd dropped the ax after clubbing the man who'd menaced Pike. And now she was cut off from Pike, hurting from a boxed ear and a bruised cheek. Plus, she was winded. A numbing ache spread through her chest, her lungs cried for air.

"Say yer prayers, gal," Grizzly growled. "Let ya go? No thankee! I want yer cunt!" Bullet-head lowered, the brute launched himself. Jenny, cat-quick, ducked under his arm, but had only managed to flee into a dead-end corner.

"Haw!" guffawed Conroy, shuffling forward.

The woman fought with the fury of madness, pummeling Conroy's massive front, but only ending up tight in his grasp. In a final attempt to turn the advantage, Jenny's hand grasped the haft of his sheathed belt knife.

With a whisper of polished steel against leather, the long blade came free. Struggling in Grizzly's grip, she drew the Bowie outward as far as she could. Gathering the last of her waning strength, Jenny jabbed downward with the sharp point.

194

In the corner of the cave where McConnell battled, the beset man strove desperately against ganged-up foes. Pain lanced through his skull and body. He tried to fight back, but the odds against him were lopsided. He gave up the effort and concentrated on dodging as many blows as he could.

Skins felt his ribs caving, and a hot, wet flow from his head wound. Dub Perkins, barrel-chested and strong, took the lead in hammering the victim. Pinwheels of fire swirled before Skins's eyes, and he grunted in pain when a rib cracked. His arms went around his head to shield it. The fireworks in his head brightened.

He fought and he lost. The sparks suddenly died, and Skins McConnell's brain sank into deep night.

Not only did Jenny stab Grizzly, she twisted the knife. Steel slid through the man's flesh until the blade ran out of inches. Conroy went rigid, agony bursting inside his chest. Still, he made another lunge, forcing the woman to drive home the blade again.

Grizzly went into a fall. Air whistled through his teeth. He relaxed his grip on the woman's arm, his jaw sagged and his gaze went blank.

"There, you son of a bitch! Teach you a lesson! Don't use bad language to a lady!"

Conroy groaned feebly, and fell dead at Jenny's feet.

* * *

Over by the cave's wide mouth the light was brighter—but the gang numbered three to Pike's one, and the big man was hard-pressed. He'd seen McConnell downed, knocked out a minute ago, and now Skins's conquerors rushed to join Ab Walsh. Walsh threw punches left and right, but Pike stepped nimbly back, hammered a blow to Bart Potter's unprotected chest. Then he seized Bart by the ears and slammed his knee up into the man's gut. Bart stumbled clumsily, gasping for breath. He collided with tough Swen Jorgensen, and both he and the Swede tumbled to the cave floor.

Pike sprang forward through the smoky air, and grabbed Potter by the scruff of the neck with his left hand. His right hand wrapped in big Swen's hair. Pike crashed the men's skulls together, felt them yield, heard them crunch. Then letting the limp, dead pair fall, he turned to face his last—most dangerous—adversary.

Walsh roared with rage and came at Pike.

This time Pike was ready, his leg muscles tensed like steel springs. He powered forward, danced aside, avoiding the Arkansan's blow. Walsh turned, his mean-eyed face surprised, and the bearded man closed with him.

Walsh had his own considerable strength. He kicked out, caught his calf behind Pike's knee and pulled the bigger man's leg from under. Pike went halfway down, then recovered himself. He pivoted as his opponent struck, a looping right, and the blow merely grazed his jaw.

Pike's retaliatory punch landed squarely, flush to Ab's cheek, and he saw Walsh's head snap to one side.

"Goddamned nine-lived bastard! I'll chop yer liver out!"

And Walsh aimed to do as promised! He'd scooped up the fallen ax, and now ran at Pike, drawing the weapon back! Pike ducked and brought his elbow up, aiming for Ab's chin. But Walsh, because his body was turning with the force of his swing, caused Pike to miss. To avoid the next vicious roundhouse chop, Pike took a step back, tripped over a dead foe and nearly went down.

Then his eye glimpsed a gleaming knife in the hand of the corpse. His hand darted and snatched up the weapon. "Now it's blade against blade, you son of a bitch!" Pike advanced, slashing with the blade, backing Ab to the cave's mouth, and then outside.

Pike followed the Ludlow's Bay man.

From here on, they'd battle on the ice-caked ledge!

The surface of the ledge was treacherous, its surface sprinkled with snow, but glass-slick underneath the powder. Walsh balanced himself, swung the ax, and the flashing blade sliced Pike's furred coat collar, raking a bloody groove into the skin it covered. Pike felt a warm trickle run down his neck. The big man ran in, slashed with his knife, and opened Ab's cheek so that crimson blood spurted. Walsh's moccasined foot slipped, Pike's did as well, and both men pitched, sprawling, into a snowbank.

Still Walsh clutched his ax. He came up with it, tried to lash out, but slipped again.

Pike got up and circled with a crouching gait, the borrowed knife clenched tightly in his fist. He jabbed at Ab's chest, but the foe ducked and the knife sliced air. Then Walsh, from his prone position, brought his legs up, drove them into Pike's side. Pike fell back, glimpsed Walsh scrambling toward him, brandishing his ax.

The tempered steel reflected dazzling sunlight.

Pike reversed the knife in his palm, and hurled the weapon.

With lightning speed, Walsh rolled aside, the knife missed, and the man went sliding down the slope. Great dark ruts were chewed in the smooth snow. Ab was out of reach, at least for now.

Damn!

Pike turned and peered upward, scanning the towering vast mountain that soared above the cave. Nearly a thousand feet of beetling, pristine snow cover. Beautiful. Beautiful as hell.

Jenny's voice close by Pike's side said, "Skins is hurt. Hurt bad."

He looked down at the woman, who was shivering, hugging herself. Her face was starting to swell, and her lower lip showed a smear of blood. "How are *you* making it, gal?"

"I'm shaky, but I'll be all right. Skins, though—"

Pike followed her into the dim cave. Stepping around the littered corpses, they made their way to their friend. McConnell lay stretched out on the rocky floor, unconscious. His chest rose and fell, but his face was sickeningly gray, waxen.

"Help me loosen his clothes," the woman said.

"Sure, Jenny. Then we'll get a fire started, put snow to melting, boil water—"

Just then the floor of the cave began to shake. A tremendous rumbling noise reached the pair, building louder and louder in volume. Pike and

Jenny turned, eyes fixed on the cave's mouth, transfixed. Downward across the mouth, blotting out all view, sheets of white cascaded, a blinding curtain. The waves of rapidly sliding snow continued to come.

A resounding *vroom-vroom* reached deafening proportions.

"What's going on?" the woman shouted.

Pike dashed for the opening, but was driven back by flying ice chips and grit. He stood motionless then, watching the sky blocked out, darkness take over. "What's happening? Ab Walsh is what's happening! The bastard somehow broke his fall, crept back up the mountainside. Got above this cave. He had that ax with him, he could've chopped a tree. Or dislodged a boulder to start the snow sliding." He slapped the cold rock wall. "Damn!"

"Then—?"

"You guessed it, gal. The worst has happened. You, me and Skins—we're trapped! By the granddaddy of all avalanches."

Chapter 34

Dark as it was in the cave, out of it and up on the mountainside the sun shone dazzlingly. Ab Walsh, hugging an ice-glazed granite rampart, squinted against blinding glare and surveyed what he'd wrought. The vast slope had been lined with spruce and aspen trees, their slender branches bowed by loads of white snow.

Now the landscape was transformed.

Monumental jumbles of gray, snow-streaked boulders stretched away and down from him. Acres and acres were dotted by half-buried, knocked-down trees, their trunks flung about like gigantic bones. And the avalanche was still alive and rampant. Shimmering, cascading waves of white still rushed downward from the spot where the man stood rooted. The wall of smothering snow flowed fast, and carried all before it.

The ground vibrated. The running mountain roared like cannon fire.

Walsh held mittened hands over his ears.

It was awesome, the devastation a man could cause by starting a boulder rolling. Walsh could no longer see the cavern mouth below. So he'd succeeded.

Pike and the woman were prisoners of the snow. Buried alive. "I win, Pike! Damn you! You'll freeze to death and rot in hell!"

His eyes lifted to the peaks overhead. His skin coat was heavy, but he'd lost his cap. In the silence that was settling in, the only movement seemed his blowing hair. The ax in his hand felt like an icicle, Walsh shivered. He'd need to get down the mountain, get himself warm before—like Pike and the woman—he faced death by freezing. Ab ventured out along an outcropping, floundered on bad footing and wrenched his ankle.

Sudden, brutal pain washed up his leg. The cold had weakened him more than he'd thought. He tried to fight off the pain, but was unable to.

His head was spinning like a child's top. He couldn't die, not Ab Walsh! Ludlow's Bay Company was going to make him rich! LeSage had promised! Behind Ab now was the hardscrabble existence he'd always known!

Walsh staggered ahead, slid back, and then both legs went out from under him, and he went tumbling. Down the steep slope he rolled, arms and legs churning. He plowed dirty residues of snow, leaving ugly black furrows. His small head sustained contusions and scrapes. Downslope from him now was the brow of a bluff, and he was rolling toward it. Trying to arrest momentum, he threw out his hands: the skin was instantly flayed off. Pain! Big pain!

Then off the great rock lip he rocketed, plummeting through the thin, cold air. He was hurtling through space, the windswept earth hundreds of feet below.

It rushed up to meet him with express-train speed.

He plowed into a snowbound slope, felt the air burst from his lungs in a shout. Incredible pain! His chest felt like a blazing fire, the result of broken-rib-ripped lungs, a mangled gall bladder, a ruptured spleen. But that hurt was matched by pain from his snapped arms and shattered hip.

The gorge floor again rushed up at Walsh.

Scared almost witless, the cartwheeling free-faller screamed.

Walsh collided headfirst with an avalanche-scoured ledge of bare granite.

Then he felt nothing but cold, as the world went dark for him for good.

Chapter 35

"Will we die from lack of air?" In the deep chill of the cave, Jenny stood slapping her arms against her sides.

"No." Pike's voice was calm. Calmer than the mountain man really felt.

Fear in her voice, the woman went on. "That snow debris buried the whole entrance. Tons of snow! *Why* won't we smother to death?"

"That's why, gal." He pointed up. A hundred feet above their heads could be seen a gleam of blue sky. The yard-square opening was at the highest vaulting of the basaltic dome. "The hole will let air into the cave, and smoke out, when we get a blaze going. The jaspers laid in plenty of firewood, at least." He stepped around the sprawled, bloody remains of Bart Potter.

Why had that boy gone wrong? he wondered.

Shrugging off gloom by sheer willpower, the big man went to fetch an armload of kindling chunks. The handful of punk he drew from his pocket was dry. Using flint and steel, he soon had a blaze going.

"Now let's tend to Skins. Help me carry him, Jenny. I can do it alone, but don't want to hurt him worse." The man and woman stretched McConnell on a bedroll near the flames. The hurt man lay unmoving.

McConnell's features were blue with cold, the moustache frozen stiff. "Should we try to get something warm into him?" Jenny looked around, spotted the Walsh gang's food hoard. There was pemmican in the pile—plus bags of rice, beans, coffee. And a moldy-appearing deer haunch.

"Warm a hurt man before feeding him. But first of all we better tend those wounds."

"Strip his clothes off?"

"Till he's buck-naked. Wash him, splint any broken bones. Use wet tobacco on the cuts. Then wrap him up tight in a buffalo robe. He's been badly beaten, but I don't think he was shot."

Jenny, feeling better in the warm, giggled. "Ain't you afraid I'll be shocked? Seeing a man totally bare-assed?"

Pike ignored the remark. "We'll do what we can for Skins, and then you better cook some grub. I'll be dragging dead bodies to the front, trying to stick 'em in the snow, pack ice around 'em. Maybe that way save ourselves from bad smells."

"Pike, has anyone told you you're not romantic?"

"I reckon *you* did. A time or two."

She peeled the shirt from McConnell's torso, and winced when she saw the bruises.

They went to work on the unconscious man, steadily and gently.

Pike and Jenny hunkered in front of the fire, devoured platefuls of shaved bacon and fried beans. The warmth had spread about the firepit, and to its far side, where McConnell lay. Skins hadn't opened his eyes, but his face was less waxy. Under the pile of robes, his torso was bandaged with buckskin strips. His left arm, which was broken, wore a splint.

He seemed to be sleeping normally, wasn't feverish. Good.

"Pike," the woman broke the silence. "We simply can't wait in this cave till the snow melts. That might not be till spring. Now, if you could climb up to that smoke hole—"

Pike rubbed the bandage on his grazed neck. "Jenny, it can't be done. The walls are too steep, that ceiling's a rounded dome. I'm not a fly or a bat. Best for us to turn in for now, get some rest— like Skins is resting. He'll be awake tomorrow, maybe have some ideas."

"Well, I *do* ache all over, and I'm drowsy."

"We've got healing to do. Sleep will tend to help it along."

She glanced at him sidelong. "Do we share a pile of robes?"

"We got to keep warm."

Pike was snuggled against the woman, dreaming, when the soft hand nudged gently, drawing him awake. The aches in his back and shoulders had almost faded to nothing. He rolled over, and Jenny's mouth came down on his, hot and writhing. Her hands roamed under his shirt, his only garment.

He caressed her body in return, found her naked under the warm robe.

"I bet I know what you want."

"Same thing as you, mister!"

Jenny reared herself, pressed her ample breasts over his face. She found his mouth, and lowered a taut nipple. He accepted the softness, tugging and sucking eagerly. Jenny cried a pleasure cry. Her hands traced along his chest, then her lips grazed a moist path to his abdomen. Found the dark nest above his groin, his long, stiff cock, which throbbed when she grabbed it.

He lay back and enjoyed the sweet sensations as the woman nuzzled and lapped. Teased his mushroom with her tongue. She straightened her young, firm legs, took his thigh between them and rubbed her wet crotch back and forth.

Her pulsing vagina opened, and his fingers found it. He caressed her love core, pressing the soft folds, fingering the velvet sheath. Her own touch grew more urgent, and she pressed his spongy gland to her joy button.

Male juices, female juices flowed, drenching their parts. Jenny threw back her head and wailed. "Now, Pike! Oh, please! Now!"

With a heave, Pike entered her.

His splayed hands gripped the woman's buttocks. Delighted with his hardness, she writhed and gasped and clawed at him. His swollen cock probed her womb, and her hips ground hard against him. She shuddered. He shuddered. He felt his belly tighten—he needed to explode.

The simultaneous orgasms, when they came, were wrenching, savage. Her head rolled from side to side, her mouth open as she reached each new peak. From extreme tension he took to quivering, felt her rock against him, suck him to her depths. She was filled.

They lay touching each other, fondling and nuzzling. He found his penis coming back to life, rapidly attaining the size and rigidity of a fireplace andiron.

"Want to try it a second time?" she purred.

"I'm agreeable."

She put her arms around him, and their mouths met in a torrid kiss. She ran her hands along his spine, down his hard-muscled buttocks that tightened at her touch. His cock had gotten hard so fast, his testicles hurt.

Pike's hands worked in circles against her skin, he positioned himself behind her, put his stiff bone at her damp warmth. She seemed to drink in the sensation greedily. His groin pressed the raised cushion of her backside.

Sounds of satisfaction rose in her throat.

Reaching back, she stroked his sexual parts, kneading him like biscuit dough. Pike's body temperature climbed, the pulsing in his veins became an insistent throb. The woman smelled good to him—musky and aroused.

Slowly, Pike eased his cock into her cleft. She began to pitch like a ship at sea, hips grinding, threatening to separate from him. As he pumped his enormous length in and out, her rocking body settled into a cadence. With each new stroke of his shaft, she squirmed and cooed and bucked.

Not surrendering an iota of her lust, she engaged him in combat, bringing him by turns to a wild pinnacle, then turning all pliant, supplicating. He roughly cupped her breasts and squeezed her nipples. She squeaked with desire. He pumped and she pumped ferociously.

She was writhing wildly on his penis, and he kissed her nape and lapped her ear. Then she was climaxing, and climaxing again, a riot of orgasms, each more intense than the last. "Don't stop," she moaned.

"I'm *not* stopping."

"Aah!" she wailed. "Aah! Aa-aaah!"

He massaged her love tab skillfully with his forefinger. By now her eyes were glazed and her head swung giddily. Finally her pulsing vagina gave its mightiest spasm, and this time he exploded, too. Hot, flooding milk from his balls shot forth, bathing her innards.

She flopped on her side. "Now we sleep."

But Mountain Jack Pike couldn't sleep. From where he lay he could look across at Skins, whose eyes were closed, whose chest rose and fell under the heavy covers. Pike hadn't wanted to fuel Jenny's fears, but he was damned if he could figure how to beat the avalanche. Facts were facts: the cave's mouth was buried under tons of snow. There was far too much to dig through. Yet if they failed to get out, they'd die. True, they had the food and wood the varmints had stored, but spring was months away. There weren't supplies enough to feed the three of them: Pike, Jenny, and Skins.

The embers finally went out, and it grew dark. Pike lay awake, even more uneasy than before. His nostrils twitched at a familiar, sour odor.

Those damned corpses were rotting.

Chapter 36

By the time daylight came again—and blue sky was visible through the roof hole—Pike knew how he'd proceed. Rising from the bedroll he pulled on his buckskins, then padded over to check Skins. He found himself being stared back at. The jolt of surprise was electric.

"Old friend!"

"Howdy, Pike."

"How do you feel?"

"Like I been through hell. Dragged by my balls. With my pecker bouncing along behind." He wagged his bandaged head, pointed to his immobilized left arm. "I reckon it's busted, all right. But you splinted it with old ramrods?"

"We've got plenty. More rifles than we can use, too. Can guess what happened to Ab Walsh's gang of cutthroats?"

Skins nodded. "Dead? By Christ, I hope so. After what they did to Blue Hand—"

"And what they did to *you*. They almost cracked your skull. Succeeded with a rib or two, it looks like."

McConnell tried a pained smile. "My skull's too thick to crack. By the way, what are we doing in here? The cave looks mostly the same as I remember, but—"

By now Jenny was awake and stirring. "Pike forgot to tell you," she said. She was buttoning her shirt over those luscious breasts, having already pulled on her buckskin pants. Her long fringes swayed as she moved. "We've been trapped by a damned avalanche. Pike claims Walsh must have started the snow sliding."

"Jesus! My headache feels worse!"

"Pike and I think there must be another entrance. And we're going to find it. Till then, we've got the gang's supplies to use, plus snow to melt and drink, wood to burn."

"Speaking of wood, I'll build up the fire. Bacon and biscuits for breakfast, Skins?"

"Sounds strengthening and tasty. Christ, I hurt everywhere. But I reckon I can chew."

"So that's the plan?"

"That's the plan."

"Not much of a plan," McConnell concluded. He touched his splinted arm and winced. "But you're right about one thing, Pike. If anything's to be done, it's up to you and Jenny. *I* ain't up to exploring dark tunnels. Maybe in a few days—"

Pike set down his empty plate, chewed the last of his biscuit. "I don't want to delay, Skins. I want us out of the cave. And awake at night, I happened to remember. Yesterday I saw a tunnel off this main chamber."

Jenny grinned excitedly. "That's right! I hid in there for part of the fight. Then I had to come out and help you boys."

"What was it like?"

"Scary and dark. And oh, yeah—deep."

"Like it runs all the way through the mountain?"

"Maybe."

"We can hope," Pike said, standing up. "But we can do more—take us a look-see now. I saw candles among the supplies, and a few other things likely to be useful." He strode to where the goods were piled. "Look!"

He held up a crockery jar.

"What is it?"

"By the smell, it's bear tallow. And tallow can be used to make torches. We wrap a branch of firewood with cloth rags, drench the wad and light it. Like this."

Pike took several minutes showing them what he meant. "You ready to start out, Jenny? Skins will stay behind, rest up and keep the fire burning."

Jenny asked, "Guns? Do we need guns?"

"We'll each carry two loaded ones. A rifle and a Kentucky pistol apiece. And we'll take knives, tomahawks, grub and torch fixings."

"Am I ready to get out of here?" she said. "I'll never be readier!"

A quarter hour later, loaded down with weapons

and other gear, the couple trudged into the hidden recess. The height of the ceiling was seven or eight feet. By the light of the torch they could see water sheening the walls.

Through the narrow passage Pike led the way, one hand holding a torch, the other his Hawken. Jenny was right at his heels. "Isn't this exciting, Pike?"

"Exciting and dangerous. That's why I'm walking in the lead."

A choking cough came from her. "Did y-you say dangerous?"

"There's a number of miscues that could happen. The shaft might branch, and we could pick a wrong way and need to backtrack. Too many branches, twisting and turning—folks could get lost. Then, there could be pockets of bad air. Or ledges that crumble, so a body falls off."

"Animals. What about wild animals? Man-eaters, maybe?"

"Like hibernating bears? Who'll get mad they're woke up? Sure, we might run up against one. But it's damned unlikely."

"We've got guns. That's why you wanted 'em along, isn't it? Protection from bears!"

"Jenny, I said—"

"Oh, I know what you said, Jack Pike!" She put a palm against his buttock, shoved him along. "Now, never mind the dangers, and let's get going. The sooner we find a way out, the better."

Pike moved more rapidly. He couldn't bring himself to mention the greatest danger of all. That they'd be unable to find an exit from this dank, foul cave. That after days or weeks, hunger would settle in. That they'd eventually die, without ever seeing again the mighty, snow-clad forests and mountains.

"It's cold. Damn it, Pike, it's cold."

The big mountain man could only nod to the troubled woman, and press on. They couldn't have been trudging through the winding corridors for more than a half hour, but already the cavern was wearing on their nerves. Gloomy and ominous, it stretched ahead and branched occasionally, like a sea creature he'd once heard tell of, called an octopus. Whenever he and Jenny came to a branch, Pike took care to blaze a trail—break off a rock spike or leave a pile of stones to mark the way back.

Skins was waiting for them, and Pike wasn't going to fail to find his way back, if he could help it.

Of course, that was a mighty big "if" . . .

It felt as if they had wound around too many bends, or come too far. The cave floor was damp underfoot, and by the torchlight Pike could see mysterious corridors leading off at angles. Still they kept to this one, the least narrow.

The claustrophobia was even getting to Pike now, more and more. What if there was no way out, or if there was, what if they couldn't find it? What would it do to a man and woman to lose their way, to feel hope eroding, to waste day after day hiking endless tunnels for a nonexistent route to freedom?

The farther they went, the lower the ceiling became.

"Pike, we're going to have to crawl."

"Then, we'll crawl. Just wait a second while I light us a fresh torch."

In less than a minute they were on their way again, Jenny going nearly flat, Pike behind with the sputtering, fuming torch. The going was hard on their clothes, and soon their buckskins were worn through at knees and elbows. "Somewhere," Jenny muttered, "there's fresh air, sunlight, trees—"

When Jenny, as she scrambled, glanced back at Pike, he could see a tautness to her features, a worried pucker to the mouth. They negotiated a passage that opened into a broad, high chamber. Water, over many centuries, had trickled and made limestone formations on ceiling and floor. In the light of the torch, the grotesque forms seemed to waver spookily.

"Pike—"

"Let's set down, rest a spell. Won't do any harm, might do some good." She sat, and he sat beside her.

This part of the cave stank of wild-beast odors. In fact, the animal smells were almost overpowering. Muskiness stung the man's and woman's nostrils.

"I don't like this place," Jenny told him.

"Me neither, gal. But we may as well go on as turn back—" Suddenly Pike's grip tightened on his rifle.

He caught sight of the enormous painter cat.

Jenny could see it, too. The couple sat frozen on their bench of rock.

The mountain lion—a male—crouched on a ledge about ten yards to the couple's right. The tawny animal was almost a full seven feet long. Blazing, yellowish eyes stared unblinking at the man and woman.

The cat's long tail switched constantly back and forth.

"Pike! What—?"

"Hush, gal! That's got to be the big painter that's been terrorizing the valley. The one that killed Summer Rain's horse. This must be its lair." The mountain man wedged his torch in a rock crevice. Then slowly, he brought his rifle up.

From the catamount's deep throat came first a rumble, then a high-pitched scream. The scream sounded like a terrified woman, only it was unearthly. Pike hoped Jenny would never have need to cut loose that way. He considered what he knew of catamounts. Wolves always attacked their prey—buffalo, deer, antelope, moose—at the rear flank, whereas bears waded right in with their claws. The mountain lion seized the throat of larger prey, and dragging the head down, snapped the neck with its strong teeth.

That's what the big cat would try to do to him.

That was why Pike sighted *very* carefully down the Hawken's barrel . . .

The cougar's tail stopped lashing.

"I'm going to shoot it, Jenny. If the critter don't die right off, I want you to skedaddle. I mean run like hell! Don't wait around for me!"

"Pike, I've got a gun, too—"

"No time for talk now!"

Pike thumbed his weapon's hammer back. *Click!*

At the sound, the cougar laid back its ears. Snarled. Came out of its crouch and sprang at him.

Chapter 37

Pike triggered off his shot.

His rifle bullet caught the catamount in the shoulder, leaving a bloody gouge in the sleek hide. In midair, the monster let out a roar. The man tried to dodge, but the creature was too fast. The cat impacted him with the full force of its body, spinning him around and sending his rifle flying from his hands. Pike and the animal went to the floor together, the heavy cougar on top and clawing.

"Good God!" Jenny Henderson screeched. But she held her ground, rifle in hand, not following the man's order to flee.

Pike fought desperately to keep the painter's fangs clear of his throat. The claws of its front paws raked his chest, doing heavy damage to the man's thick hide coat.

The man, wrestling the powerful cat, attempted to roll it over on its back, but failed. He seized the monster by the neck with both hands, and squeezed with all his strength. The cat threw itself from side to side with power and fury, its talons ripping Pike's clothing and Pike's skin. Blood spurted in rivulets.

Finally the cat pulled free of Pike's grip, but the man lashed out with his feet, kicking. The cat, thrown off balance, rolled along the cave floor and caromed off a limestone outcropping. Pike took advantage of the chance, yanked the Kentucky pistol from his belt.

"Jenny? You still here? Damn it, I told you to clear out—"

The catamount, ears back and snarling, was again creeping forward toward Pike. Blood oozed from the groove the rifle ball had chewed in its front. The animal's amber eyes glowed with hate.

Pike stood his ground, let the catamount come closer. He raised the pistol with both hands and triggered, but from the firing pan came a mere hissing *pffft*—a flash in the pan. The gunpowder was damp from the cave air. Without waiting for the cat to spring again, Pike brought the gun's butt down hard between the furry ears.

The cougar hissed and spat and slithered backward.

Pike swung the weapon a second time, but now it glanced off the cringing cougar's foreleg. Then the monster rushed in, swiped with a massive paw, scoring Pike's right biceps.

Pike winced at the pain, but made no move, expecting the cat to spring. It, too, seemed to be waiting.

"Pike!" he heard Jenny Henderson croak. "Glance my way!" The big man did so, saw the woman clutching a tomahawk—one of those she'd lifted from a dead member of the Walsh gang. She tossed the weapon, and Pike plucked it out of the air.

Just then the catamount leaped. Pike dodged to let the cat fly past, then spun and hurled himself. As it thrashed underneath him, he succeeded in pinning it by locking his knees about its middle. The hindquarters of the monster kept surging, as Pike dealt the panther's nose a glancing tomahawk blow. The man's arm lashed out again at its moving target. The panther's roar was now directly in his face, horrifying and deafening. The stink from the gaping, eighteen-inch jaws almost made Pike gag.

Again Pike struck with the tomahawk, this time connecting soundly. The fur-coated face was cleft crosswise, and one eye popped out to dangle by the optic nerve. The cougar roared its agony, brain matter geysering, and then the animal's muscles spasmed a last time. It dropped to the stone floor and lay motionless, the once-magnificent fur now filthy and gore-splashed.

"Is it dead?" Jenny asked, creeping up.

"Damn right it's dead." Pike leaned against the wall, his shoulders for once sagging. His breaths came in great wrenching gasps.

"Lordy, but your coat's in shreds. Here, let me look at that claw damage to your chest. Hmm. Not too bad. It isn't even bleeding much. But I wish I had clean snow to wash off the blood."

Pike automatically went about reloading his guns. "Me, I wish I had a swallow of tangleleg," he grunted

"The cougar scratches must hurt."

"I can stand that. I want to celebrate."

"You guessed what I already guessed—right?" Jenny flashed a harried-but-bright smile.

"Here's what I figure: if the painter slept in here, it was able to get in and out. That means there's a cave entrance, for sure! And my bet is, it's not far from where we stand!"

The way onward when they left the cougar's lair seemed easy going. Jenny was cheerful; Pike was cheerful. Their escape from the cave was close. They trucked along a low-ceilinged tunnel, Jenny carrying the torch.

Then the passage grew narrower and steepened. "Maybe this isn't the way the painter came," Jenny fretted.

"We've got to try it," Pike said. As the tunnel tightened and steepened, they had to drop to hands and knees again. The couple was forced to arch their backs, brace themselves against the walls to keep from sliding backwards. Their fingers dug at wet, slick limestone. Pike's and Jenny's arms knotted at the effort.

"Damn!"

"Just when we thought our troubles were over!"

Then, when the passage was at its tightest, Pike saw light ahead—daylight!

There was a gap in the rock, all right—but was it large enough? Pike was a giant of a man. He staggered forward. "Come on, Jenny!"

When he reached the opening in the gray stone, his heart skipped a beat! The opening *was* big enough, even for his massive frame. He squeezed through and stood to full height.

The sky was blue, the surrounding peaks were white, except where dotted with green trees. The temperature was frigid. Pike wanted to gulp the fresh air, yet realized that if he did, his lungs would be seared with cold.

"We made it," Jenny whooped. "Now all we need is to go fetch Skins."

"*And* hike down the mountainside, try and find our horses, get to the trappers' camp—"

She didn't let her excitement die. "But we can do all that, Pike! I know it!"

"I know it, too."

Part Four
The Furs

Chapter 38

A sunshiny bright morning in early spring was dawning on Eagle Valley. The warm breeze from the south, blowing now for days, had melted almost all the ice on the streams and ponds: the water glistened like a million diamonds. Pike stood on the heights above the camp, watching the mountainsides turn from sunrise pink to the pale greens of freshly leafed-out forest.

Today the trappers would move out with their pack train, fifty horses strong, no less. Pike had given the order yesterday, and the fur-bundling and gear-packing had gone forward in a rush. The season's harvest had been bountiful. The packs of pelts had been prepared in the usual way for sale at post or rendezvous: sixty otter pelts to the pack, eighty beaver, two hundred muskrat.

Many, many bundles of the "soft gold" would ride the X-frame saddles down from the high country. And each horseload would sell for hundreds of dollars at the trading post—a handsome sum.

Now Pike saw Skins McConnell limping toward him, much recovered from his ordeal after the fight with the Walsh gang. He raised his right—unsplinted—arm in a wave. "Black Feather sends word that his Snake People are packed up, ready to ride."

"Thanks for the word, Skins. What about Whiskey Sam's crew of men?"

"Horses loaded. The fellas under Elijah and Gap-Tooth are all set, as well."

"And the women?"

"Summer Rain and Jenny decided to keep company on the trail. I like the notion. Figure you will, too."

Pike nodded, cast his hawk-sharp eyes around a last time. "I like the idea fine. I reckon this is good-bye to Eagle Valley. Can't say as I'll miss the place."

"After Black Feather's braves found Walsh's body at first melt, I felt a lot better. With Ab out of the way—plus his gang and that big painter cat—the valley wasn't bad. Plenty of furs for the taking, and we took 'em."

"Yeah, you're right, Skins." Pike tramped over to his saddled black, standing next to McConnell's chestnut. Pike swung aboard, balancing his Hawken in his left hand. McConnell mounted also, and as he settled in the saddle he pushed his hat down on his brow.

Pike reined his mount around, and rasped, "Now the job's getting the pelts to Graybull. Flanagan's expecting our pelts."

"One thing worries me," McConnell said. "Bap-

tiste LeSage and his Ludlow's Bay bush-lopers—
they're sure to be waiting."

"Along the trail? With bushwhack plans?"

"I'd bet on it, Jack. The furs aboard our train—
they're worth a fortune."

Pike trotted his horse toward where the party was
formed and ready to move out.

"I'd bet on it, too, Skins. In fact, I'd lay odds!"

Alone among his warriors, aboard his best pony,
Black Feather thought hard about the mission
ahead. He couldn't believe the party wouldn't run
into terrible danger. Was the prophecy going to be
fulfilled for his people—the one foretold in the
nightmare about the owl?

Only time would tell.

The party negotiated the pass and started down-
mountain, stringing out in a long line. They came
on Sheep Creek, which melting snow had flooded,
and had to cross farther downstream than the high
ford. This took them off the familiar path, and Pike
decided to circle widely, try a high-mountain route
he recalled from years before.

On the first night they camped high in the mountains, and on the second through the fourth days
they veered east and traveled south-facing slopes.
They crossed valleys of thick spruce, dotted with
outcroppings of limestone.

The horses weren't sure-footed on loose rock,
and getting down the bluffs strained men's and
women's nerves. Once Pike chose a ledge path that
dead-ended, and the riders had to dismount, turn
the animals about, and lead them back. But they

227

were getting down into less-thin air. They hurried across a fir-grown swale and into a clearing: this was ambush country, and Pike ordered all to keep sharp watch. The fourth night they stopped beside another fast-running creek. Along the green banks the horses would find enough graze.

They unloaded the animals, cooked a deer that one of the Snakes had brought down with bow and arrow. Dancing Quail and the other squaws had gathered edible roots, but the white men preferred biscuits made with flour. Eventually everyone turned in, well-wrapped in their bedrolls. In the pitch-darkness well past midnight, Pike heard McConnell creep to Summer Rain's soogan.

Skins was getting better every day, for which Pike was glad. Now Jenny, alongside Pike, stirred. He rolled against the woman and slept.

Chapter 39

It was morning when they rode into trouble.

Pike, as usual, rode at the column's lead, the long line of pack animals strung out behind. Behind him he could hear the creak of saddle leather, the monotonous hoofbeats, an occasional trapper's oath. As they wound along a switchbacking downslope trail, all looked and sounded perfectly normal.

Pike cast his eyes eastward to a row of distant rock pinnacles, trying to see what lay along the path ahead.

Trees blocked the big man's view, but as he rode on, he came to a point where the cedars opened. Pike popped a handful of parched corn into his mouth. Good chewing. Magnificent peaks rose in the distance on all sides. Then far below, a dark cloud of wheeling birds erupted from the trees.

Birds that had been frightened by something?

Pike raised his hand in a signal. All the drivers of the packhorses reined up. A tiny spot of yellow was moving among the trees a quarter of a mile ahead. Pike leaned forward in the saddle and looked closer. What had he seen?

And then another moving something followed the first. And then another.

"Skins, look down there!"

"A line of horses, by God! Riders. And leading packhorses without packs. LeSage's little private army?"

"I can't think of anybody else who'd travel in the open in Blackfeet country. Pass word back to our men."

Pike and McConnell sat their mounts, resting their rifles across their saddle pommels. "If we could recognize LeSage for sure—it'd be our cue," Pike told his sidekick. "Then we could be damn sure that outfit's up to no good."

Far below, the strangers gigged their horses under dense timber. Minutes passed. Then movement could be seen again.

McConnell and Pike strained their eyes. There was something familiar about the jasper in the lead. "That's LeSage, I'd bet my leg!"

"Pass the word to our men! They should see to their priming!"

Pike himself uncapped his powder horn, freshened the priming in both his rifle and pistol, then jammed the pistol back under his belt.

By now most of the trappers had ridden up to sit their horses, faces grim. Gap-Tooth Williams and Whiskey Sam Benedict spat tobacco juice and swore. "All right, here's what we'll do," Pike told them. "The men I name in a minute will dismount and go after the bastards. Elijah, you'll be in charge of one party, and I'll lead another. Black Feather, you'll be at the head of your braves."

"What party do I go with?" McConnell asked.

"Skins, you'll stay here with the women and horses. Your leg's not yet a hundred percent."

"Son of a—"

Pike turned to talk to the subchief. "Black Feather, when you get to the flat, fan out, station yourselves along the trail. They outnumber us at least three to one, and they'll fight like devils."

Elijah Rowe asked, "When do we open fire?"

"You'll hear me shoot my Hawken off."

Pike grinned and stroked the big gun.

LeSage trotted his leggy roan, his ugly face crazed-looking, but eager.

"How much farther till we set up th' ambush?" the rider beside him said. "Another half day, or a day?"

"*Merde!* I told you! When I see the best spot to lay in wait for Pike and his trappers!" Then, as an afterthought, he commented, "Ab Walsh, he never sent word to me when the snow melted. That I don't like."

"You don't reckon Walsh got killed?"

LeSage's single eye appeared the texture of blood-streaked bone marrow. "Prob'ly. I don't reckon he'd be inclined to pull a double-cross. Ludlow's Bay Company's payin' him well. And 'twas him told me Pike's plan, after all—Eagle Valley, the free trappers working in cahoots."

Marcel DuPont wagged his beard-shagged head. "If Walsh be dead, that is too bad."

LeSage disagreed. "No real harm, so long as he told no tales. Never mind the company. About me. About how I changed my plan, and now aim to capture and burn Fort Graybull. Slaughter the defenders. To hell with Ludlow's Bay influence! *Baptiste LeSage* will take over all the fur trade in the Bitterroots."

DuPont grinned wickedly. "Ya got balls, Baptiste—that I'll admit. Carvin' out yer own, for real, fur empire—"

"I accept your congratulations, *mon ami*. Here, let's share brandy from my flask."

LeSage took the first pull from the vessel, his larynx jumping like a rat in a trap.

They rode in silence for a time, but for the clink of bridle chains, the creak of saddle leather. LeSage and DuPont rode at the head of sixty heavily armed fighting men. Then Baptiste burst out, "One thing I insist on, Marcel. We'll attack the trappers soon, snuff out many lives. But Mountain Jack Pike, he's mine to kill—and scalp. He, and Flo Lipscomb, and that other white woman."

"Oui, Monsieur Booshway."

LeSage's face was hideous, the grotesque scar more wormlike livid than usual. His grin was a grimace under the great hooked nose.

He belched. The alcohol on his breath wafted.

"That other white woman, whose name I never found out. But I think of the pleasure I'll take from her, *mon ami*. A great pleasure for me, a great suffering for her!"

"Yeah, Baptiste? What ya aim t'do—?"

"First of all, we capture her alive. Then, after the gunplay, I rape her, and then all my men rape her. Finally, we string her up by the ankles from a tree."

DuPont gave a lewd chuckle. "Yeah, booshway, that's good. And *then* what for the white doxy?"

A guffaw rolled from LeSage's throat. "I keep the last for my little secret, no? One hint, Marcel, and only one hint." The scar-faced man leered.

"She's got plenty of hair to be peeled by us, no? And more than only head hair!"

Pike ghosted downslope, around boulders and under thick-branched trees. He moved silently on moccasined feet through clumps of underbrush. The big man stopped, signaled the men at his heels, and they stopped, too, dropping into crouching positions.

The spot where they waited overlooked the trail. Pike scuttled up behind a giant deadfall and flopped flat.

He scooted his rifle forward and rested it across the log.

The only sounds were the wind and some far-off bird cries. Then, close by, a horse's hoof kicked against a stone. More hoofbeats followed and became louder. The animals were moving at a walking gait. Then Pike saw the first horse, and swaying in the saddle a scar-faced, one-eyed man.

Baptiste LeSage.

The ugly face couldn't be mistaken.

LeSage was speaking to a bush-loper who rode alongside, and the Canadian booshway's voice carried clearly. "We'll attack the trappers, snuff out many lives. But Jack Pike, he's mine to kill—and scalp. He . . . white woman . . . pleasure—"

"Yeah, Baptiste?" The other man egged his boss. "And that's—?"

". . . after the gunplay . . . rape . . . string her up . . . ankles—"

"Jesus!" Pike growled, under his breath.

LeSage laughed boisterously. "She's got plenty of hair to be peeled by us, no? And more than only head hair!"

That was when all hell broke loose!

Jack Pike's cheek pressed against his rifle's maple stock. Lightning-like he drew a bead and triggered. The flint snapped and the pan flared. The Hawken let loose a roar, belching a huge cloud of white smoke.

But just at that moment, the roan pranced and LeSage shifted his seat. Pike's shot whizzed by his ear. The man behind LeSage was punched from his mount, arms flailing, and crashed to the trail.

Rifles alongside Pike cracked and popped, and more bush-lopers were slapped from their horses. Pike used his pistol to blow Marcel DuPont into eternity. Spooked horses bucked and reared, but several enemies managed to bring their own guns into play.

Before Pike's discharged gun could be reloaded, no fewer than three riders galloped his way, shouting and brandishing rifles.

A heavy lead ball slammed the log near Pike's head. The foes shouted as they charged, and the big man got to his knees, used his teeth to uncap his powder horn. The enemy riders closed the distance, reining their horses one-handed as they pointed their rifles.

Just off to Pike's right, "Coon" Satterlee's Bedford County flintlock boomed. The ball plowed the first rider's stomach, and he somersaulted backward off his horse.

More rifles on both sides roared fusillades.

By now another rider closed in on Pike. Pike lowered the Hawken's stock, grasped the barrel and upended his powder horn. Charged the barrel with a hefty load. But Pike still had to fumble with the lead ball, linen patch, and ramrod.

The rider loomed now, blocking out the sky. "*Sacrebleu*," he yelled. "Swine! You die!"

Pike was splashing fine-grained priming powder into his rifle's pan. But the rest of his time ran out.

The bush-loper's face lit triumphantly. The horseman's range was point-blank.

"Pike! Watch yer ass!" Coon hollered.

Pike dropped the powder horn, leveled the Hawken, jerked his trigger without taking time to aim.

The big rifle thundered and spat.

Chapter 40

The Hawken erupted both noise and white, acrid smoke.

Pike's enemy staggered backward, smears of blackish burned gunpowder coating his front. The shaft of the shattered ramrod stuck from between his ribs.

The jasper clawed at his chest as the blood gouted and splashed: a crimson bib. Gasps burst from his mouth, his legs shook and his eyes bugged out. Somehow, though, he kept his feet. He raised his musket and prepared to shoot.

"Pike! Don't let him kill ya!"

Pike smoothly drew his tomahawk. He raised it high, his stance a throwing stance. Snapped his arm forward, his whole tremendous weight behind the throw. The tomahawk flipped as it flew; then the sharp blade cleaved Pike's foe's face. Gone was the long, straight nose. The man's eyes popped out, and rolled on the ground. The impact knocked the dead man down. His weapon clattered on the rocks.

Everywhere now, guns boomed and tomahawks clattered. War whoops filled the air. Gap-Tooth's voice rang out, "Give 'em hell, fellas! Damn their hides! They'd ha' done fer us!"

A man with his chin blown away bounded past Pike. "Yow! Yow! Yow!" The Canadian could still scream loudly.

Trappers stood their ground, firing and reloading. Rifle balls whined like crazed hornets. Gouts of turf were chewed from the earth. Riders yanked viciously at their reins, jerking their animals' heads, vaulting from their saddles. Yelps of pain vied with shouts of fury. Elijah Rowe heard a meaty *smack*, and a paint horse went down, shrilling its agony.

Rowe and free trapper Bix Frawley teamed up to meet a charge by Baptiste LeSage and followers. The mountain men sprang from cover, charged a wooded hillock. Frawley's slug smacked into flesh, and sent Antoine Fuster reeling, bleeding. The man cursed in English, in French, in the Blackfeet tongue.

A shot tore Frawley's arm half off. Rowe was in sore danger—and that was when Black Feather ran up.

Dashing ahead of his warriors, the Snake flung his five-foot war lance. The flint tip hissed past the head of LeSage. The booshway spun, fisting his French flintlock pistol. Lesage triggered and missed, then leaped out of the way of a swung war club.

Baptiste ran like a scared rabbit, pell-mell into the forest.

237

Across the glade, Pike heard a mushy sound, like that of a melon splitting. Someone's skull had been crushed by a blow. Indians were running and white men were running. A foe bore down on him, hand ax waving. Pike sidelonged and rolled. Jumping up, he freed his skinning knife, spun, saw Rowe's familiar capote, its owner swinging his emptied rifle.

Figures advanced, retreated, lunged. Pike yelled, "Hey!" and a giant adversary turned toward him, charging. Three arrows appeared in the foe's back: *thwack! thwack! thwack!*

Blood gushed from the man's mouth. Mighty Gray Wolf of the Snake tribe waded in. The downed man's scalp was ripped free with a *squish.*

Then, Pike could see, all the rest of LeSage's band had fled. "Steady, boys," Pike called. "They won't be rushing us again for a spell."

The ground was littered with dropped weapons. The bodies of horses and men. Pike retrieved the Hawken, but the ramrod was gone.

Gap-Tooth loped up. "Seen what happened to your 'rod. Why not take one o' theirs? Find one whose size'll match yore old 'un!"

On his other side, Whiskey Sam intoned sternly. "Some of 'em got away."

Pike nodded. "Expected some would. Let's see, count how many dead? One of our men, six of theirs. Shit! *Most* of 'em hightailed! LeSage among 'em!"

"Hell, booshway. Tomorrer's another day."

"That's what worries me, Gap. Next time they won't be easy pickings!"

* * *

A day and a half later, miles farther along, Pike reined in, McConnell at his side.

"Hear that?" Skins said. "A rider!"

"Black Feather, by God! Back from his scouting trip."

The subchief trotted up on his brown-and-white painted pony, the eagle feathers on his headband shining. He wiped a hand across his porcupine-quilled shirtfront. "Ho, He-Whose-Head-Touches-the-Sky! Black Feather greets you!"

"Ho, Black Feather, my friend! What has the great chief seen ahead along the trappers' path?"

The old warrior spoke in his halting English. "Many, many of your white-eyes enemies. They lie in wait along the only trail, where it passes between tall rocks. They can shoot down on us, and there is no cover. A very bad spot to ride through. Many, many of us will be killed if we try!"

Gap-Tooth Williams straddled his old bay, listening. "Damn me for a porcupine, Pike! How we gonna carry down our plunder?"

Pike thought a moment, frowning. "Wait. I just may have an idea. I seem to remember a big, fast stream that runs down that canyon. A river almost?"

The Indian nodded, thumped his chest. "There is a river. Runs fast. Rocks out where the current is strong. Waterfalls, rapids."

"But two or three log rafts just might get through—right?"

A grin overspread the subchief's brown face.

"I see your plan, He-Whose-Head-Touches-the-Sky. And it is a good plan."

It took a day to chop the trees and trim the branches off. Another to lash the logs together, stow the fur packs and supplies. Pike toiled mightily among the men, chopping, lugging, and barking crisp orders.

Once as he rested, leaning on a stump, Jenny walked up to him. "You're sure it's a good idea, this dividing your force?"

"It's the choice that seems best to me, gal. Le-Sage's scouts, they'll see the rafts with the furs shooting past 'em downstream. Chances are, they'll ride to cut us off. That'll spoil their bushwhack, leave the trail unguarded so Skins and you and a few others can slip the horses through. Our separate parties can meet up afterwards at the canyon mouth."

Jenny gnawed her lower lip. "Won't there be a fight?"

"Damned right! A rip-roaring shoot-out!" Jack Pike grinned. "I'm betting we win. What are you betting?"

The corners of the woman's mouth turned up. "Well, naturally I'm backing Jack Pike and his friends. A hundred percent. Man, haven't I seen you in action before?"

The trappers finished up work just shy of sundown. Most ate and turned in, but Pike and McConnell took the first sentry watch. They hunkered on a ridge overlooking the camp, as a drizzle of rain spat down from the night sky. "You think this raft-ing plan of yours'll work?" Skins wondered aloud, huddling in his buffalo robe.

Pike snorted. "Why wouldn't it work?"

"Hell, a hundred things could go wrong. LeSage is fucking loco, and plumb kill-crazy. Elijah told me that, who saw him in action in that last fight. Then, too, there's more of them than us, and they've got firepower. Plus, Jack, there's the river. It's unpre-dictable as hell. It's the spring season, and the wa-ter's at flood—"

Pike slapped his friend's back. "Skins, we've been through a lot together, right?"

"Right."

"There's risks to everything a man does in life. We've seen that again and again, along the trails we've rode."

"Damn it," McConnell grunted. "I want to be in on this next fight, too. Ride a raft with you and the fellas. Swap hot lead with the thieving sons of bitches!"

Pike touched Skins's arm, now worn in a rawhide sling. "I value you, Skins, and I do know you can shoot one-handed. But somebody's got to guide the women downtrail, and getting the horses past the lopers—that's going to take a damned good man. Without that, the rest of it's no use. Do I need to say anything more to you?"

Skins shook his dampened head. "You don't need to say more, Jack."

Pike climbed to his feet, his hat dripping rainwa-ter from the brim. "Then, our lookout hours being over, let's haul ass and turn in."

They trudged down to camp, and joined their women in their bedrolls.

Everybody was up early, and those picked by Pike to ride the rafts swarmed aboard. Shadows of tall pines fell across the flood-swollen river, a tributary of the far-distant, downstream Yellowstone. McConnell, Jenny and Summer Rain stood on the mud-slickened bank. The nighttime rain had passed off, and the sun peeped through breaking clouds at dawn.

Jenny stared out at the rushing torrent. Where the waters now violently raged, during the summer months a placid stream ambled. She rose on her tiptoes and waved. "Good luck, Pike!"

"Thanks, Jenny. Be seeing you again soon. By nightfall, most likely!"

Pike boarded the largest raft of the three—the one that would float in the lead—and felt a moccasin sole slip on the wet logs' surface. Then the big man shouted the command, "Cast off!"

Into the raging waters the pole-wielding trappers shoved their makeshift crafts. The rafts were instantly swept along on the rushing brown current.

The waters churned and bobbed the raft. Pike planted his feet, balanced himself. There was danger, sure, but he relished it. It meant getting the furs past LeSage, and a good part of the distance toward Fort Graybull. And it meant getting the furs into Tim Flanagan's hands so the trader could buy them.

Abruptly the raft heaved and started to revolve. Tough "Mad" Mel Melrose, standing aft as steersman, hollered out. "Hang on t' yer poles, boys! Don't let the craft turn broadside! Keep yer asses dry!"

Pike knew the savvy trapper was right. A sudden swing of the raft broadside would pit the strength of the rawhide lashing against the full force of the flood.

In this rough water, capsizing would mean death.

Pike crouched with the Hawken in one hand and a pole in the other. He squinted ahead at the surging, foaming rapids the rafts were bearing down on.

Chapter 41

In a few yards shooting down the swift stream, the trappers saw the river getting rougher. The rafts bobbed and bumped together, and the one Pike rode fell away suddenly, almost spinning. The squat trapper at Pike's side was thrown off his feet. But he didn't go overboard. Pike grabbed him by a sleeve and pulled him back.

"Don't turn turtle! We need every man!"

"Thanks, Pike. Saved this coon's bacon, y' did!"

With a whiplike force the raft suddenly swerved, threatening to throw more men off their feet. Gap-Tooth gripped the shoulder of Ike Booth, but the violent rocking knocked them both down. Mountain men cursed, but kept gripping their poles, not letting them be jerked from their hands. Pike's raft was catapulting downstream, all right. But it still wasn't out of control.

The world spun faster and faster. An enormous

bundle of furs broke its tie-downs, starting to slide. Pike dashed up, and heaved the burden back in place.

The raft narrowly missed a rock, nearly heeled over.

"Hang on, boys," Pike yelled. "Hang on!"

Something tugged his pantleg, and a bee-buzz whistled past his ear. Christ! Flying rifle balls?

A split second later, he heard the shots fired from the tree-lined bank. A trapper screamed in pain, flipped into the foaming flood and was sucked down. Unfortunately, he was the steersman. Pike's raft shuddered and crunched: it had collided with the second raft. Pine logs splintered, and the vessels drifted into a wild spin. The raft tipped crazily . . .

More gunshots came from shore, spouting smoke puffs from a score of muzzles. Geysers erupted in the swift, brown tide. Above all, there was the river's raging roar.

All around, the water boiled unmercifully.

Baptiste LeSage urged his horse between the mud-slick walls of the ravine. His men were laying down steady fire, and the men on the rafts had dropped flat.

"Downstream! They're going to run aground!" the scar-faced one whooped, leaping from the roan's back and landing running. He bolted down the incline to the muddy riverbank. Brown waters lapped at his fine-stitched moccasins.

"Baptiste!" someone shouted warning. "Look out, that raft! It's coming aground!" And the raft did so, disgorging a clutch of Indians—war-whoop-ing, painted Snake warriors. LeSage pointed and fired his buffalo gun. An Indian's head exploded, and he back-flipped, dead.

LeSage hurled away the discharged rifle. People on every side were scattering. Everyone was shooting now, as fast as they could. A bush-loper rested his rifle on his left forearm and fired. Hit nothing. The subchief Black Feather planted his feet, fired three arrows with incredible speed. One snatched off Mike Forester's cap; LeSage's right-hand man staggered, disoriented. A brave called Flying Loon collided with the man, who grabbed him and shoved him backward, hard. He hit the flinty ground and rolled to his feet.

Flying Loon crashed a bone club into Forester's skull, bursting it.

"Booshway! *Mon dieu!* Get down!"

The Snake drew another arrow, nocked it, and drew back the string of his bow. LeSage dove, and the flint-tipped arrow flew, nicking his cheek. He was bleeding, but still alive. *"Merci*, Prosper! *Merci!'* Then he saw the trappers storm off the second grounded raft, Jack Pike in the lead.

"The *blancs*, men! Kill the *blancs!* Then the furs, they'll be all ours! We'll be rich, *mes amis!* Rich!"

Jean Moreau aimed his club-butt Charleville musket. In the sights he found none other than Elijah Rowe.

A warrior dashed in boldly, splitting Moreau's skull with a swift tomahawk stroke.

Firearms banged. Powder smoke fogged the air. The Indians rallying, LeSage cursed, searching to find a fallen gun. He bent down, and an arrow dug turf in front of him. Ten or twelve of his men lay

246

n heaps, others had fled, the rest gave and received ire. LeSage swung the long gun he'd scooped up, clubbed a trapper with the cast-iron buttplate. Then moving quickly, he drew his skinning knife and slashed four rapid strokes.

His victim scalped, Baptiste belted the hank of grisly skin and hair.

Pike stormed up the muddy bank. Rage was blazing fire in his dark eyes. The first man he sought was LeSage, but he couldn't get at the scarred Canadian. Before he'd dashed two steps from the surging river, he was confronted by a gigantic bush-loper. Pike raised his Kentucky pistol and dropped the flint. The foe's face was ripped open by the ball, blood and pink froth spraying down the man's buckskins. Choking with his blood, the Canadian folded like a dropped accordion.

Pike was rushed at by a second foe, but he spun around and dealt the man a mouthful of knuckles. The man recovered and lashed, sledging with right and left, managing to connect. Church bells clanged in Pike's skull, although it wasn't worship time. He mustered his strength to retaliate, gave a mighty grunt and threw a left hook. He ducked his adversary's uppercut, slammed the bulky gut of his opponent.

Canuck Rafe Bedlam half turned, but Jack Pike was all over him, raining blows. Then Pike was tackled and borne to the ground. Both men rolled along the soggy bank.

Pike caught hold of his opponent's wrist and slammed it against a rock until the man lost his hold. Then he momentarily kicked free. The pair traded blows, then locked together again, this time hurtling down the bank and into the river.

Pike caught a hasty breath, then was dragged under. The current was strong, his enemy was strong, and tried to hold his head beneath the surface. Pike struggled, reached out and caught a handful of hair, yanked the foe close. Pike fought clear of the water, sputtering, and clipped the bushloper with a hard right to the jaw. Pike shoved him face-down into the mud, then held him long enough for him to shudder and go limp.

Then it was the next foe, and then the next; Pike's tomahawk was out and wreaking mayhem, death.

Throughout the entire width of the canyon, powder smoke stank and formed a veil. Pike glimpsed LeSage mere yards off, holding his ground, flailing with a knife the size of a short sword. Rifle balls whizzed past Pike, slammed into trees and men. Some went down shrieking; some went down, killed where they stood.

As Gap-Tooth Williams fought LeSage, the Canadian cut loose with a series of slashes. Gap-Tooth reeled back, his throat cut from ear to ear. LeSage sprang over the corpse, knife in hand. Black Feather ran up, his gnarled war club swinging, but LeSage drove him back. Ludlow's Bay man Joe McMurphy fired, and the Snake lurched away, howling.

There was a scuffle farther up the river's bank. Most guns emptied now, the battle was joined man-to-man, hand-to-hand. Directly ahead of Pike, four men lay in spreading blood puddles. Ugly wounds flowed crimson. One trapper's abdomen lay open, intestines spilled in slimy coils. Another's head was half torn off, a gaping skull oozing pale gray brain stuff.

Baptiste LeSage stood spouting curses. His scarravaged face glistened with the sweat of killing.

Jack Pike's arm flew up, and he charged.

The men met, almost knee-deep in soft riverbank muck. LeSage swung his blade in a vicious arc, missing Pike, but halting him. "And so Baptiste meets Jack Pike! The dog who stands in the way of my fur empire! How sweet to kill you! Killing you, *cela va tout seul! So, allons!*"

LeSage slashed out. Pike saw the flash in his enemy's hand come up, plunge down, and a sharp pain bit into his side. Pike twisted around, caught the Canadian's arm and hauled him powerfully in. LeSage screamed and screamed again. Pike knew he'd dislocated the man's shoulder.

The two men's faces were inches apart. LeSage's sweat had turned to cold sweat. Fear widened the Canadian's one eye. "I saw you kill Gap-Tooth," Pike hissed. "And I don't doubt that you hired Walsh, and are behind the deaths of Flo, Rufus, and Blue Hand! And the beating given Skins McConnell, nearly crippling him for life!" Pike spun the man, took him in a bear hug, hoisted him high in both hands and brought him down with all his strength.

The man's spine broke across Pike's knee, a crisp, dry *crack*.

LeSage bellowed out horrendously, then followed up with a chorus of coughing shrieks. Pike caught his foe's hair in his left hand, and Baptiste's own gleaming knife flashed in the sun. Pike chopped powerfully once, twice, a third time. At the third stroke, the ugly head separated. Pike dropped it and kicked it aside. It lay in the wet grass, blood oozing from the neck stump.

It was suddenly quiet in the narrows of the canyon. Pike filled his lungs with great breaths, turned and looked about. There were bodies of brigade men, bodies of free trappers sprawled grotesquely in death. But a good many trappers were on their feet, hobbling about, nursing their wounds or their *compadres'* wounds.

A half dozen Snake warriors circulated, taking scalps, their knives flashing and slashing as they reaped the bloody trophies. Black Feather looked up and saw he was being watched. Striding over to Pike, he stood before the big white man, arms folded across his chest.

Pike spoke first. "Black Feather, your warriors are brave. Your medicine is strong. Thanks for your help in defeating these evil men."

"I know my medicine is strong," said the chief. "I knew of this killing time from a dream that came to me. My people are glad to fight for He-Whose-Head-Touches-the-Sky."

The Indian turned and walked off, not looking back.

Pike lifted his shirt, and peeked at the knife slice in his side. It was superficial. He winced and let the buckskin fall back in place. Then he came out with a loud shout. "How do we stand, men?"

"Alive and kickin'—most of us!"

Elijah Rowe ambled across the grass, eyes alight and smiling grimly. "We really slaughtered 'em, Jack Pike. Look at all their dead. And those we didn't kill are scattered to hell and gone. Means th'end of LeSage, and the end of the brigaders' threat. Ludlow's Bay Company won't cause more trouble. Too costly. They've lost the war. So Tim Flanagan and Fort Graybull—they're saved!"

"It's true, ya know, Pike," Whiskey Sam put in. "Saints be praised, we had ya on our side."

Pike said the only thing he could think of. "Let's get the fur bundles that got busted repacked, and back on the rafts. Shove off as soon as we can. Skins and the Indian squaws, the kids and Jenny will be at the canyon mouth, waiting with the horses."

Rowe summed it up, "Amen to that!"

Epilogue

The setting spring sun cast long shadows across the wooded, flower-scented canyon mouth. Skins and the women had pitched camp early. It was a beautiful land, the sandstone rock faces alive with glowing color.

The rafts came, being poled out of the gentle current. The reunions were made, the deeds and deaths calmly reported.

The trappers sat on the ground and filled their stomachs. Smoked pipes. Nipped rum or trade whiskey.

Slept.

Pike and Jenny had laid their bedroll in a place apart. The glade was surrounded by blossoming shrubs, the air fragrant, the small creatures scurrying in the dark underbrush.

"I'm glad the fighting's over, Pike. I'm glad you're back safe. I knew you'd make it."

"I knew it, too."

"Still, let me show you I want you."

This night was a moonlit night. He could see her form, silvered by the sky-borne disk. Standing, she let down her hair, which cascaded down her shoulders.

"A right pretty sight," Jack Pike said in a husky voice.

"I know what you like, Pike. Let me show you that I know."

Her eyes came up to meet his, as her long fingers undid her buckskins. They fell in folds around her feet, and she kicked them aside. Meanwhile, Pike shed his own clothing that had seen such hard use. The man watched as Jenny's breasts swung free, her hips gave a sensuous twitch. She stepped close and knelt before him, her supple body entirely naked. Her thick, luxurious triangle caught a moonbeam, and shone, causing Pike to grin. She smiled mysteriously in turn.

Reached out.

Touched his chest.

He felt the old, familiar stirring in his loins. Her gaze fell to his stirring vibrancy, and her tongue flicked across her lush lips.

She came against him, and he let her bear him down, her tender body pressed hard against him. Her long legs wrapped his waist, her glistening wetness tracking his hard, flat abdomen.

His index finger touched a budding nipple.

"Ah, yes, that's the way! Aah, Jack Pike! Aa-aah!" Her legs slid wide to receive him. He penetrated, and she writhed as he drove deep, sinking effortlessly into her hot cauldron.

She cried out, surged up violently, welcomingly Snakelike she twisted, husky mewings going to full-throated groans. Her hands found his back, the fingernails dug at his skin. Then the tremors started, and she lurched under this man, this hard man, whose pulsing gristle probed her core.

Her hips throbbed and her pelvis gyrated. The cadence reached a crescendo. She spasmed wildly

She was reaching a peak of sensation. Her head thrashed on her neck, her eyes, open, rolled. Her lips drew back from pearly teeth. She shuddered and arched her back. Her butterflying hands toyed with his buttocks, crack, and balls sack.

He ministered to her, plowing deep.

She orgasmed. He orgasmed, and his seed pumped out, gouting. They flopped apart and lay quite still.

"Enough?" he asked.

"Enough for now." She sounded drowsy—very drowsy.

"If you wake and want more—"

"I know. You'll oblige. I thank you for that."

He was dozing, too, atop slick softness. The softest bedroll he'd used. "What's this we're lying on?" he queried. Then he caressed the softness and he knew.

"Furs," she chortled

"Beaver furs?"

"*Prime* beaver furs. You trapped 'em yourself, Jack Pike."

"I'm going to want you, woman, halfway through this night."

"That'll be good. Now, sleep."

Across the draw, a horse nickered and stamped.

"Did you hear something, Skins?" asked Summer Rain softly.

"A horse. Only a horse." The man shifted, lying against her in the bedroll folds.

"How you feeling, Skins?"

"Good."

"But I bet I can make you feel better."

Then the woman curled her body, and her head was between his legs. Soft kisses teased his sexual member. Her tongue roamed the length of stalk, and it turned rigid. She encircled his acorn with her warm, wet lips. Suckled, intent on delighting the man.

"Honey, you win your bet! *You sure do!*"

His body bucked.

Her body bucked.

The moon sailed the star-strewn sky.

WALK ALONG THE BRINK OF FURY:

THE EDGE SERIES

Westerns By GEORGE G. GILMAN

*Available wherever paperbacks are sold, or order direct from th
Publisher. Send cover price plus 50¢ per copy for mailing an
handling to Pinnacle Books, Dept. 706, 475 Park Avenue Sout
New York, N.Y. 10016. Residents of New York and Tennesse
must include sales tax. DO NOT SEND CASH. For a free Zebra
Pinnacle catalog please write to the above address.*